"So tell me about this* new *Phelix Bradbury."

"There's not a lot to tell," she replied. "I worked hard—and here I am."

"And that covers the last eight years?" Nathan queried skeptically.

He halted, and she halted with him, and all at once they were facing each other, looking into each other's eyes. And her heart suddenly started to go all fluttery, so that she had to turn from him to get herself together. She supposed she had always known that this—"the day of reckoning"—would come.

She took a deep breath as she recognized that day was here.

Dear Reader,

Congratulations, Harlequin! Sixty wonderful years! I have been writing for Harlequin for half that time—thirty years—and have so enjoyed being part of this great company.

Coincidentally, it was sixty years ago that I was in Davos, Switzerland, where *Falling for Her Convenient Husband* is mainly set. I was in hospital there for some months and always meant to return. However, many years passed, and it was not until Peter, my husband, asked would I like to celebrate our fortieth wedding anniversary there that a return became fact.

Davos has changed greatly since I was first there, but I was still able to pick out places I knew, and had the most wonderful time renewing my acquaintance with the small town. It was a joy. And it was because of that inner happiness I experienced that I had such pleasure in writing *Falling for Her Convenient Husband.*

I hope to have shared some of that pleasure with you, and that you will enjoy reading this book.

Best wishes,

Jessica Steele

JESSICA STEELE

Falling for Her Convenient Husband

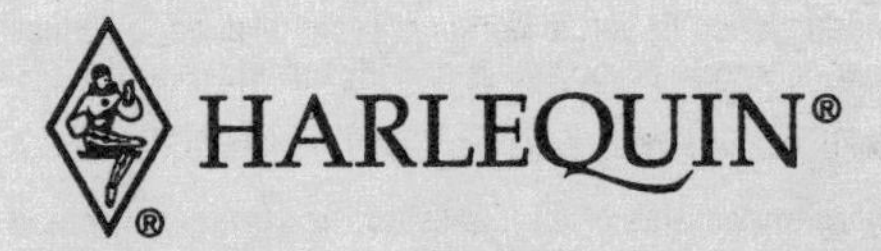

TORONTO • NEW YORK • LONDON
AMSTERDAM • PARIS • SYDNEY • HAMBURG
STOCKHOLM • ATHENS • TOKYO • MILAN • MADRID
PRAGUE • WARSAW • BUDAPEST • AUCKLAND

Recycling programs
for this product may
not exist in your area.

ISBN-13: 978-0-373-17573-4
ISBN-10: 0-373-17573-6

FALLING FOR HER CONVENIENT HUSBAND

First North American Publication 2009.

This edition published by arrangement with Harlequin Books S.A.

www.eHarlequin.com

Printed in U.S.A.

Jessica Steele lives in the county of Worcestershire with her super husband, Peter, and their gorgeous Staffordshire bull terrier, Florence. Any spare time is spent enjoying her three main hobbies: reading espionage novels, gardening (she has a great love of flowers) and playing golf. Any time left over is celebrated with her fourth hobby: shopping. Jessica has a sister and two brothers, and they all, along with their spouses, often go on golfing holidays together. Having traveled to various places on the globe, researching backgrounds for her stories, there are many countries that Jessica would like to revisit. Her most recent trip abroad was to Portugal, where she stayed in a lovely hotel, close to her all-time-favorite golf course. Jessica had no idea she'd become a writer, until one day Peter suggested she write a book. So she did. She has now written more than eighty novels.

Get ready to be swept off your feet by perfect English gentlemen!

Harlequin Romance® brings you another fabulous, heartwarming read by bestselling author

Jessica Steele

Jessica's classic love stories will whisk you into a world of pure romantic excitement....

Praise for the author:

"Jessica Steele pens an unforgettable tale filled with vivid, lively characters, fabulous dialogue and a touching conflict."
—*Romantic Times BOOKreviews*

CHAPTER ONE

PHELIX had not wanted to come. Oh, she loved Switzerland, but her previous visits had always been in winter when the skiing was good.

Yet now it was September and, apart from the remains of winter's snow on some of the highest peaks, there was no snow. In fact the weather was sunny and beautiful. And here she was in Davos Platz, having arrived last night—and still feeling very annoyed because, in her view, there was no earthly reason for her to be there.

It was 'business' her father said. What business? She was a corporate lawyer working for Edward Bradbury Systems, her father's company. But she could not for the life of her see why any lawyer, corporate of otherwise, would need to attend a week-long scientific, electronic, electrical and mechanical engineering conference!

'I can't see why I have to go,' she had protested when her father had informed her of the arrangements he had made.

'Because I say so!' Edward Bradbury had replied harshly.

At one time she would have accepted that. Would have had to accept it, she knew. But not any longer. Not blindly, and certainly not without question. In the past she had been forced to accept every edict her control-freak father uttered. But not now. So, 'Why?' she challenged. It had taken a long while for her to get where she was, to get to be the person she now was. There was nothing left now of the weak and pathetic creature she had been eight years ago. 'If it's work related, I could understand a need. But for me to spend a week in Switzerland with a load of scientists who—'

'Networking!' Edward Bradbury chopped her off, but unbent sufficiently to explain that there had been whispers for some while that JEPC Holdings, one of the biggest names in the industry, were about to outsource a vast amount of their engineering. He had now, personally, along with the top brass from other competing companies, been invited to make the same Swiss trip next week, when the top men from JEPC would be flying in for a round of exploratory talks, give a general outline, and chat with the various highest of executives. 'It will mean millions to whichever company gets the contract,' he stated, money signs flashing in his eyes. Phelix still did not see, since as yet there was not a sign of any contract, why she had to go. 'I'm sending Ward and Watson with you. I want you all to keep an ear to the ground; listen for anything else going on that I need to know about.'

Duncan Ward and Christopher Watson were both scientists and wizards when it came to electronics. But Phelix doubted that there would be anything going on apart from a load of boring old speeches. It made her feel a little better, though, that the two scientists, both men she liked, would be there too.

'I've booked you into one of the very best hotels,' her father stated—as if that was an inducement!

'Duncan Ward and Chris Watson too?' she asked.

'Of course,' he replied stiffly. And that, as far as he was concerned, was that.

It was not that, as far as Phelix was concerned. The very next day she went to see Henry Scott, her friend and mentor, and who was also the company's most senior corporate lawyer. Henry was nearing sixty and, through their various conversations over the years, she had learned he had been a very good friend to her mother.

He must have been an excellent friend, Phelix had long since realised. Because it had been Henry that her mother had called on the night she had died. The night she had taken all the cruelty she could take from her domineering husband and had attempted to run away from him.

Phelix's thoughts drifted back to that dreadful time. Back to that awful night. It had been a foul night when, pausing only to make that phone call and to throw some clothes on, Felicity Bradbury had fled her home. When she pieced everything together afterwards, Phelix thought that her mother must have seen car headlights coming towards her in the storm thrashing about overhead, and had run out into the road in the blinding rain. It had not been Henry, and the car driver had stood no chance of not hitting her. Henry had been held up by a tree that had crashed over in the storm and which had blocked the road. By the time he had found another route and reached her home, he had been acquainted with the news he had arrived too late. The police had waved him on.

But while he had not been in time to help Felicity, he had made sure that her daughter would not ask for his help in vain.

It had been Henry who, almost eight years ago now, had aided Phelix when she had decided that she wanted a career of some sort. He had taken her seriously to suggest, 'Being a corporate lawyer is really not as dull as it may sound.'

'You think I could become a lawyer?' she'd asked, for one of the few times in her listless life feeling a surge of excitement at the thought.

'I know you could—if that is what you want. You're bright, Phelix. It will mean a tremendous amount of hard work, but we'll get you there, if indeed law is what you fancy doing.'

And she had rather thought she did fancy a career in law. She had recently—no thanks to her father—had quite a lot to do with lawyers. She had found them upright and trustworthy which, having discovered the duplicity of her father's nature at first hand, was more than she could say for him.

He, needless to say, had not cared for the idea of her taking up legal training—most probably because it was not his idea. But by then she'd been on the way to receiving ten percent of the very substantial sum of money her grandfather—the same type of hard nut as her father—had left her.

'I said *no*!' Edward Bradbury Junior had declared vociferously. 'I forbid it!'

She had still been in awe of her father in those days. But, having only a short while ago been party to the biggest untruth of all time, she had again felt the stirrings of breaking free from the chains of his life-long dictatorship over her.

'Actually, Father, I'm eighteen now, and no longer require your permission,' she had dared.

He had taken a step nearer and, purple with rage, had looked as though he might strike her. And it had taken every scrap of her courage not to cower back from him, but to stand her ground.

'I'm not paying for your years of training!' he had spat at her, enraged.

'You don't need to," she had answered, still watching out for his clenching and unclenching fists at his side. 'I've been to see Grandfather Bradbury's solicitors. They tell me—'

'You've done *what*?'

He had heard, she was not going to repeat it. 'They were most surprised to learn that the letters they had sent me had gone astray.' Not half as surprised as she had been to hear the full contents of her grandfather's bequests to her—nor the conditions imposed. 'But what happened to my private and confidential mail is no longer important. I now know I have sufficient money to fund my own studies.'

Edward Bradbury had thrown her an evil look. She'd always been aware that he had no love or liking for her, and in the days when it had mattered to her she had wondered if it would have been different had she been the son he had so desperately wanted. But his love and liking had never been there, and had he ever loved her mother that love had died stone cold dead when she had failed to produce the male heir he'd so badly wanted.

'Would you like me to leave home?' Phelix had been brave enough to volunteer, more than hoping he would say yes.

She supposed she had known in advance that he would say no—she was the buffer between him and their housekeeper, Grace Roberts. In actual fact Phelix knew that Grace had only stayed on after her mother, the gentle Felicity, had been killed, for her sake. Edward Bradbury was under no illusion that if his daughter left then Grace, who was only a few years away from retirement anyway, would leave too. He enjoyed Grace's cooking, enjoyed the fact that his shirts were laundered exactly as he liked them, enjoyed that his home was run on oiled wheels—he had not the smallest interest in spending his time trying to find a new housekeeper who would only measure halfway up to Grace's standards.

'No, I wouldn't!' he had reported bluntly, and stormed out of the room.

Phelix came out of her reverie and supposed she ought to make tracks for the Kongresszentrum. But she had little enthusiasm for the day's events: a general introduction and getting to know some of the people. 'Networking' as her father called it.

She was more than a little off him at the moment. Had she not made that phone call to Henry from the airport before she had left yesterday she would probably not have known until today exactly why her father was so insistent that she attend.

'Do I really have to go, Henry?' she had asked the senior lawyer.

'Your father will play hell if you don't,' he'd answered gently. 'Though…' He'd paused.

'What?' Phelix had asked quickly, sensing something was coming that she might not be too happy about.

'Um—you're coming back a week tomorrow, right?'

'I'll come back as soon as I can. Though I suppose I'd better stick it out until then. My father and all the big chiefs will be there from a week Wednesday—thank goodness I don't have to be!'

'Er—not all the bigwigs are leaving it until next week,' Henry informed her kindly—and suddenly her heart lurched.

There was a roaring in her ears. No, she definitely wasn't going! Though, hold on a minute, her father would never send her on this mission if he thought for a single moment that *he* would be there.

'Who?' she asked faintly, wanting confirmation and urgently.

'Ross Dawson,' Henry supplied, and a whole welter of relief surged through her.

To be followed a few seconds later by a spurt of annoyance at yet another sign of her father's underhandedness. Ross Dawson was a few years older that her own twenty-six years. He was the son of the chairman of Dawson and Cross and, it had to be said, had a 'thing' for her despite Phelix telling him frequently and often that he was wasting his time.

'Do me a favour, Henry?'

'I've already done it.' He laughed, and she laughed too. All too plainly Henry Scott had known that she would check in with him before she left London.

'Where am I staying?' she asked, loving Henry that, without waiting to ask, he had transferred her hotel booking.

'A lovely hotel half a mile or so from the conference centre,' he replied. 'You'll be more than comfortable there.'

'You've cancelled my other reservation?'

'Everything's taken care of,' Henry assured her.

She rang off a few minutes later, knowing that her father would go up the wall if he ever found out. But she did not care. It went without saying that Ross Dawson would be staying at the hotel she had previously been booked into—her father would have got that piece of information to him somehow.

Deciding she had better be going, Phelix checked her appearance in the full length mirror. She'd had her usual early-morning swim, in the hotel's swimming pool this time, and was glowing with health. She stared at the elegant and sophisticated unsmiling woman who looked back at her, with black shiny hair that curved inwards just below her dainty chin. She used little make-up, and did not need to. She wore an immaculate trouser suit of a shade of green that brought out to perfection the green of her eyes.

Phelix gave a small nod of approval to the female she had become. There was nothing about her now—outwardly, at any rate—of the shy, long hair all over the place, gauche apology for a woman she had been eight years ago. And she was glad of it—it had been a hard road.

Having hired a car in Zurich and driven to Davos, she opted to walk to the conference centre, and left her hotel quietly seething that her father so wanted an 'in' with Dawson and Cross that he was fully prepared to make full use of Ross Dawson's interest in, not to say pursuit of her to that end. He was obviously hoping that by spending a week in close proximity of each other, with limited chance of her avoiding Ross, something might come of it!

She wouldn't put it past her father to even have telephoned in the first instance on some business pretext, and then casually let Ross, a director of Dawson and Cross, know that his daughter would be in Davos for a whole week.

She felt hurt as well as angry that her father, having sold her once, cared so little for her he was fully prepared to do it again. Over her dead body!

But, thanks to Henry having got wind of what was going on, he had been able to forewarn her, and at least do a little something to limit the time she had to spend with Ross. Not that she didn't like Ross. She did. She just had an extreme aversion to being manipulated. And, in the light of past events, who could blame her?

She knew that her father had been having a liaison with his PA, Anna Fry, for years. She wished he would concentrate his attentions more on Anna, and leave his daughter out of his scheming.

As Phelix neared the Kongresszentrum she saw other smartly dressed representatives making their way towards the entrance. She would be glad to see Chris and Duncan, she realised, and hoped nobody else would wonder, as she had before Henry had tipped her off, what possible reason she could have for being there. At least she had been spared the surprise of seeing Ross Dawson unexpectedly.

She made her way inside the building, hoping there were no other unexpected surprises waiting for her on this trip.

'Where did you get to?' She turned to find that Duncan Ward and Chris Watson had spotted her coming in and had come over to her. 'We looked high and low for you last night. Reception said you hadn't checked in.'

It was gratifying to know that they had been concerned about her. 'I should have let you know,' she apologised. 'I'm sorry. I thought I'd prefer a hotel a bit further away.'

'As in I might have to put up with you two talking shop during the day, but I want some rest from it in the evenings?' Chris grinned.

'Not at all.' She laughed, and did not have a chance to say anything else because someone was calling her name.

'Phelix!' She looked over to where Ross Dawson was making his way over to her. 'Phelix Bradbury!' he exclaimed as he reached her.

'Hello, Ross,' she replied, and was about to make some comment with regard to his act of being surprised to see her there when, even as Ross kissed her on both cheeks, she caught a glimpse of a tall, dark-haired man standing with a blonde woman and another man. But it was the dark-haired man that held Phelix riveted. She felt a deafening silent thunder in her ears, but even as she tried to deny that *he* was here after all, it took everything she had to keep her expression composed. She glanced casually away, but not before she noticed that he had been looking at nowhere but her!

Her insides were all of a jangle. She had not seen him in eight years, and only twice before then, but she would know him anywhere! She had been just eighteen then, he twenty-eight. That would make him thirty-six now.

Phelix began to get herself more of one piece when she realised that, thankfully, he could not possibly have recognised her. She was nothing remotely like the awkward and, in her view, late-developing teenager she had been then. But that was it—she was out of here!

But, having grown a veneer of sophistication, even if her insides were now feeling like just so much jelly, Phelix knew she could not just simply cut and run. But she wasn't staying, that was for sure! As soon as she possibly could, she would tell either Chris or Duncan that she had forgotten something, had a headache, a migraine, athlete's foot—she didn't care what—and was going back to her hotel. From there she would make arrangements to fly back to England.

Hoping against hope that he was a figment of her imagination, she found she was irresistibly drawn to glance over to him again. It *was* him! He was tall, but even so would have stood out from the crowd of people milling around.

She slid her glance from him to the other man standing with him, and on to the close to six feet tall glamorous blonde woman. His girlfriend? Certainly not his wife.

Oh, heavens, he was looking her way again. Phelix flicked her glance from him. She was not unused to men giving her a second look, so knew his second glance was no more than passing interest. But, apart from his female companion, herself and several other women, the conference seemed to be a predominantly male affair.

She tried to tune in to what Ross and the other two were

babbling on about, but when she felt as much as surreptitiously glimpsed the man leaving his companions, so her wits seemed to desert her.

But—oh, help—he seemed to be making his way in her direction! Dying a thousand deaths, Phelix prayed that he was making his way elsewhere, or that if he was perhaps coming over to say hello to Ross, that Ross would not think he had to introduce them; the name Phelix was a dead give-away.

He halted as he reached them and her mouth dried and her heart raced like a wild thing. 'Ross,' she heard him greet Ross Dawson, and saw him nod to Duncan and Chris. And then he turned his cool grey eyes on her. How she remained outwardly calm as, for the longest second of her life, he studied her, she never knew. And then casually, every bit as if he had seen her every day of his life for the past eight years, 'How are you, Phelix?' he asked.

Her throat was so dry she didn't think she would be able to utter a word. But the poise she had learned since she had last seen him stood her in good stead. 'Fine, Nathan,' she murmured. 'You?'

'You know each other?' Ross asked.

'From way back,' Nathan Mallory drawled, his eyes still on her. She guessed he couldn't believe the evidence of his vision; the change in her from the frightened timid mouse she had been eight years previously to the cool, collected and polished woman who stood before him now.

'You're here for the conference?' she enquired, and could have bitten out her tongue for having asked so obvious a question.

'One of our speakers had to drop out. As I intended coming this way, I thought I might as well come early and fill in for him.'

She smiled, nodded—she knew darn well his name had not been down on the programme as one of the speakers. She, knowing he was likely to be in Davos next week with the other heads of businesses, had scrutinised the list of speakers very thoroughly before at last bowing to her father's insistence that she come this week as part of the Edward Bradbury Systems entourage.

'If you'll excuse me,' she managed, striving with all she had to hold down the dreadful feelings of anxiety that were trying to get a hold—she hadn't felt like this in years! 'I think I have to register in.'

Somehow or other she was able to make her legs take her in the direction she wanted them to go. And later, having had no intention of still being there but somehow having been swept along, she was in a seat, listening without taking in a word of what the introductory speaker was droning on about.

She had by then started to recover from seeing Nathan Mallory again after all those years. As well as being tall with dark hair, Nathan was handsome—quite devastatingly so. A man who could have any woman he chose. But Nathan Mallory—she drew a shaky breath—was *her* husband! She, for all she went by the name Phelix Bradbury, was in actual fact Mrs Nathan Mallory. Phelix Mallory. Oh, my word!

As she twisted her wedding ring on her finger—the marriage band he had put there—her thoughts flew back to more than eight years ago. She ceased to hear the speaker's voice and was back in the cold, cheerless home she shared with her father in Berkshire. She was no longer in the conference hall, but was in her father's study, back before she had met Nathan.

Her grandfather, cold and forbidding Edward Bradbury Senior, had died shortly after her mother. Phelix had missed her warm and loving mother so much, and later realised that, perhaps needing warmth and comfort at that time, she had been ready to imagine herself in love when Lee Thompson, their gardener's son, home on vacation from university.

It seemed as though she had always known Lee. She had always been shy with people, but he'd seemed to understand that as their romance blossomed.

Though he'd left it to her to seek her father out in his study and tell him that she and Lee were going to marry.

'Marry!' her father had roared, utterly astounded.

'We love each other,' she had explained.

'You might love him—we'll see how much he thinks of you!' Edward Bradbury had retorted dismissively. And that had been the end of the conversation—and the end of her romance.

She had seen neither Lee nor his father again. When Lee had not phoned as he had said he would she had telephoned him, and had learned that his father had been dismissed from his job and that Lee had been bribed—for that was what it amounted to—to sever all contact with her.

She had been too shocked to fully take in what Lee was saying. 'What do you mean—my father will pay off all your student loans?' she had protested.

'Look, Phelix, I'm in hock up to my ears. I was mad to think we could marry and make a go of it. We'd be broke for years! You're not working and—'

'I'll get a job,' she'd said eagerly.

'What could you do? You're trained for nothing. Any money you'd be able to bring in would be nothing at all like as much as we'd need to keep us afloat.'

That was when a pride she hadn't known she had started to bite, and she had taken a deep breath. 'So, for money you'd forget all our plans, all we ever said? All—'

'I have no choice. I'm sorry. I shouldn't be talking to you now. I'm risking the bonus your old man promised me if I—'

'Goodbye, Lee,' she had cut in, and had put down the phone.

After that she hadn't cared very much what happened. But a few days later she had been able to accept that, her pride feeling more bruised than her heart, that she had been more fond of Lee than in love with him. And that in fact what lay at the base of her wanting to marry him was more an urgent desire for change of some sort. More a need for some kind of escape from this—nothingness. For the chance to leave home, the chance to get away from her intimidating father.

And, since it was for sure Lee had not been in love with her either, she'd realised that any marriage they'd made would probably not have lasted. Not that she had seen her father's actions as doing her a favour. She had not. She'd still wanted to get away. But she supposed then that she must have been living in some kind of rose-tinted never-land, because when she'd got down to thinking about leaving and striking out on her own, she had known that she just could not afford to leave. She could not afford to live in even the cheapest hostel. And as Lee had more or less stated—who would employ her?

Another week went by, but just when she had started to feel even more depressed, her father summoned her to his study. 'Take a seat,' he invited, his tone a shade warmer than she was used to. Obediently, she obliged. 'I've just been advised of the contents of your grandfather's will,' he went on.

'Oh, yes,' she murmured politely, wondering why he was bothering to tell her. Grandfather Bradbury had been as miserly as his son, so probably had a lot to leave—but not to her. In any event, she was sure that anything he left was bound to have some ghastly condition attached to it.

'Your grandfather has been very generous to you,' her father went on.

'Really?' she exclaimed, surprised, Grandfather Bradbury had never shown any sign that he knew she existed when he had been alive.

'But I'm afraid you are unable to claim your quite considerable inheritance until you are twenty-five,' he enlightened her. The hope that had suddenly sprung up in her, died an instant death. Bang went her sudden joy at the thought that she could leave home and perhaps buy a place of her own. 'That is, unless…' her father murmured thoughtfully.

'Unless?' she took up eagerly.

'Well, you know he had a thing about the sanctity of marriage?'

To her mind he'd had more of a thing about the iniquities of divorce. He'd had a fixation about it ever since his own wife had walked out on him and, despite all his best efforts, had ultimately divorced him. He had passed his loathing of women breaking their wedding vows down to his son. Phelix's mother had confided in her one time when Edward Bradbury had been particularly foul to her how she had wanted to divorce him years ago. He had gone apoplectic when she'd had the nerve to tell him—delighting in telling her that if she left him she could not take their daughter with her. 'When you're eighteen,' she had promised, 'we'll both go.' And, until that last desperate bid when Phelix had been seventeen, she had stayed.

'Er—yes.' Phelix came out of her reverie to see her father drumming his fingers on his desk as he waited for her to agree that his father *had* had a thing about the sanctity of marriage.

'So—he obviously wanted you to be happy.' Her father almost smiled.

'Ye-es,' she agreed, knowing no such thing.

'Which is why a clause was inserted in his will…' Naturally there was a clause—possibly some snag to prevent her claiming her inheritance even when she was twenty-five, '…to the effect that if you marry before you are twenty-five you will be eligible to receive ten percent of the considerable sum he has left you.'

'Honestly?' she gasped, her spirits going from low to high, then back down to positive zero. Oh, if only this had happened a couple of weeks ago. She could have married Lee and claimed that ten percent and have been free! Well, not entirely free. Only now did she fully accept that she was glad her romance with Lee had gone no further. Marriage to him would have been a big mistake.

'Your grandfather plainly did not want you to suffer financial hardship in any early marriage you made.'

'I—see,' she answered quietly.

'And how do you feel about that?'

Her father was actually inviting her opinion about something? That was a first. 'Well, I wouldn't have minded having a little money of my own,' she dared. With her father forbidding her to take any lowly job which would shame him, he made her a tiny allowance that, at best, was parsimonious.

'We'll have to see if we can't find you a suitable husband,' he, having paid off her one chance of marriage, had the nerve to state.

It was the end of that particular discussion, but less than forty-eight hours later he had again called her into his study and invited her to take a seat.

'That little problem,' he began.

'Problem?'

He gave her an impatient look that she hadn't caught on to what he was talking about. 'The husband I said I'd find for you.'

'I don't want a husband!' she'd exclaimed, appalled.

'Of course you do.' He overrode her initial protest. 'You want your inheritance, don't you?' he demanded. 'Ten percent of it represents a considerable amount of money.'

'Yes, but—'

'It goes without saying that the marriage will be annulled before the ink is dry on your marriage certificate,' he had bulldozed on. 'But that certificate is all I need to take to your grandfather's solicitors and—'

'Just a minute,' she dared to cut in, 'are you saying that you've found a man for me to marry so that I can claim that ten percent?'

'That's exactly what I'm saying.'

She couldn't believe it and stared at him dumbfounded. 'Is it Lee?' she asked out of her confused thoughts.

'Of course it isn't him!' Edward Bradbury snapped.

'But—but you have found someone…'

'God Almighty!' her father cut in, exasperated. But then, obviously counting to ten, 'Yes, that's what I've just said.'

Her tutors had said she had a quick brain—Phelix wondered

where it was when she needed it. 'You're saying that as soon as I've got that—um—marriage certificate that the solicitors want to see, I can divorce—er—this man?' She wasn't going to marry anybody! Besides, her father hated divorce—there was something fishy going on here.

'You won't need to divorce him. Since you'll never live with him, an annulment will suffice.'

In spite of herself, with freedom beckoning, Phelix had to own to feeling a spark of interest. Even perhaps the small stirrings of a little excitement.

'How old is he?' she asked, telling herself she was not truly interested, but not relishing the idea of marrying one of her father's Methuselah-like cronies.

'I've checked him out. He's twenty-eight.'

That spark of interest became a flicker of flame. Twenty-eight? That was all right. She could marry and claim that ten percent, and… 'And he, this man, he's willing to go through a form of marriage with me so that I can claim some of my inheritance?' she questioned. Even while wanting to get away from the environment she lived in, she discovered that she did not trust her father enough to go into this blindly.

'That's what I've just said,' he replied tetchily.

At that stage Phelix had not known just how diabolical and underhand her father could be if the occasion demanded it. But, even so, something just didn't seem to her to tie up.

She started to use what her teachers had said was her good brain. 'What is in it for him?'

'What do you mean, what's in it for him?'

Phelix had no idea of her potential. All she saw was that she was a dowdy, unemployable newly eighteen-year-old, with little to recommend her. And while it was true that by the sound of it her marriage would be annulled as quickly as made, she could not see any man willingly marrying her just because her father asked him to.

'Does he work for you?' she asked, suspecting that some poor man was being pressured in some way to do the deed.

Edward Bradbury's thin mouth tightened at having his slip of a daughter daring to question him. 'He and his father have their own scientific electronics company,' he answered shortly.

She knew she was making her father angry. Indeed knew she should be jumping at this chance to have her own money. But, 'I don't get it,' she persisted.

'For heaven's sake!' her father erupted on a burst of fury. But he managed to control himself to state more calmly, 'If you *must* know, I heard a whisper that Nathan Mallory and his father are in a hole, financially. I approached the son and said I'll bail him out if in return he'll do this small thing for me.'

Her father was helping out a competitor? She found that hard to believe. On the other hand, as her need for freedom gave her a nudge and then a positive push, what did she know about what went on in big business?

'You've said you'll give him some money if—'

'Not *give*!' That sounded more like her father. 'I've said that in return for him marrying you—a marriage he will not be stuck with—' thank you very much '—I will that day hand over a substantial cheque, a loan repayable two years hence. Now, anything else you need to know before…?'

By the sound of it she would be doing this Nathan Mallory as much of a favour as he would be doing her. That made her feel a little better. 'He—er—knows it isn't permanent?' She found she needed to qualify. 'The marriage, I mean. You're sure he knows…'

Her father did not attempt to spare her feelings but, as harsh as he more normally was, told her forthrightly, 'I've seen a sample of the fashionable beauties he favours—take my word for it, he'll be at his lawyers annulling your marriage before the first piece of confetti has blown away.'

It had not turned out quite like that. Nor had there been any confetti. In fact it had turned out vastly different from the way Edward Bradbury had had in mind. He had thought they could be married by special licence and it would all be over and done with within a week. But in actual fact they'd had to appear at the register office in person, and give fifteen clear days' notice of their intent to marry.

So it was that, three weeks before the proposed marriage date, Phelix had presented herself at the register office and met for the first time the man she was to marry. Had she been hoping that her father would be there to ease any awkwardness, then she would have been disappointed. He had an 'important business meeting.' Why would he need to be there, for goodness sake!

'How will I know him?' she'd asked anxiously.

'He'll know you.'

From that she'd gathered that her father had given him a description of her. As it appeared he had, for a tall dark-haired man had been there a minute after her and had come straight over to her. 'Hello, Phelix,' he'd said, and she had almost died on the spot. Already, aged twenty-eight, there had been an air of sophistication about him. Oh, my heavens—and she was going to marry him!

'Hello,' she'd answered shyly, knowing she was blushing, but calming herself by remembering that this was not going to be a marriage, just a ceremony.

'We seem to have a minute or two to wait. Shall we sit over here?' he'd suggested, his tone cultured, well modulated.

Lightly he touched a hand to her elbow and directed her to a corner of the room which for the moment they had to themselves. She wanted to say something, anything, but even if she could have thought of anything remotely clever to say she felt too much in awe to say a word.

But not so him, and it appeared, while being perfectly civil and polite, he wanted there to be no misunderstanding of the reasons why they were both doing what they proposed to do.

Because without further delay, he asked, 'You're quite happy to go through with this, Phelix?'

Shyly she nodded. 'Yes,' she answered, her voice barely above a whisper.

'And your reasons are as your father stated?' he pressed, clearly wanting everything cut and dried before he committed himself further.

'My gr-grandfather… Um, I can't claim my inheritance from my grandfather until I'm twenty-five. But if I marry I can have ten percent of it,' she began, her voice growing stronger. 'And—er—the thing is, I'd quite like to have some money of my own.'

'You're thinking of going to university?' Nathan enquired.

'No,' she replied, feeling it would be disloyal to reveal that her father had vehemently vetoed that suggestion long since.

'You don't work?'

She blushed again. How could she tell someone who must obviously respect her father that her father was so controlling that anything she suggested, or her mother when she had been alive, had always been very firmly trodden on by Edward Bradbury?

'No,' she repeated. And, fed up with herself that she seemed to be totally spiritless, 'I believe you have financial considerations too, for going through with this?' she said.

Nathan Mallory looked at her then, taking in her long pulled-back hair that revealed her dainty features, observing her splendid complexion, seeming to drink in her face with his steady grey eyes on her wide green ones. 'It will be years before I'm financially in a position to marry for real,' he stated. He was serious still as he dotted the last i and crossed the last t. 'You understand, Phelix, that our marriage ends at the register office door?'

'That will suit me perfectly,' she responded primly. And suddenly he had smiled—and she had fallen a little in love with him.

CHAPTER TWO

A BURST of applause brought Phelix back to the present. 'That was pretty good, don't you think?' Duncan Ward, seated next to her, brought her the rest of the way back to the world of commerce.

'I'll say,' she responded, having not taken in a word.

'Coming for coffee?' called a voice from the aisle. It was Ross Dawson who had detached himself from the group he was with.

Phelix turned to her two colleagues. 'Shall we?' she asked. Chris Watson adopted a bland expression, knowing full well he had not been included in Ross Dawson's invitation.

'I'm so dry I couldn't lick a stamp,' he accepted.

A few minutes later Phelix was waiting with Duncan while Chris and Ross went to get them coffee.

'Are you staying the full week?' Duncan asked. He and Chris had flown out on an earlier flight, and this was their first chance to catch up.

'My father thinks it will benefit the company if I stay for the end of speeches get-together on Monday evening.' She still couldn't see how. Though her urgent need to bolt of a couple of hours ago did not now seem as urgent as it had. Plainly Nathan, after coming over and asking 'How are you?' while being perfectly happy to acknowledge that he knew her, had no intention of telling anybody that he was her husband any more than she had.

She glanced to her left as Ross and Chris joined them—her eyes seemed somehow to be drawn in that direction. Nathan was there in her line of vision, talking to the tall blonde.

With her insides churning, Phelix flicked her glance from him. It seemed to her then that Nathan Mallory had always had some kind of effect on her. Right at this moment she again felt like taking off. But, having discovered over the last eight years that she had far more backbone than she had up to then always supposed, she made herself stay put and smiled, laughed when amused, and generally chatted with her three male companions.

'Have lunch with me?' Ross asked as they made their way back to their seats.

'Sorry. I've some work I want to look through.'

'You can't work all the time!' he protested.

Sitting listening to speeches, even if she didn't take in a word, hardly seemed like work to her. 'There's no answer to that,' she replied, smiling gently at him. It wasn't his fault that on the man-woman front he did nothing for her.

'Dinner, then?' he persisted.

She almost said yes if it included Chris and Duncan. But from their point of view they probably wanted to let their hair down away from the boss's daughter.

So she smiled. Ross was harmless enough. 'Provided you don't ask me to marry you again, I'd love to,' she agreed.

'You're hard-hearted, Phelix. If ever I catch up with that mythical husband of yours, I shall tell him so.'

'Seven o'clock at your hotel.' She laughed, and glanced from him straight into the eyes of Nathan Mallory. He was no myth.

She smiled, acknowledging him. For a split second he stared at her solemnly. And then he smiled in return—and her heart went thump!

Phelix was in her seat, determined not to let her mind stray again. The current speaker was a bit dry, but she concentrated on key words—'state of the market' and 'systems and acquisitions'—and still couldn't see what she was doing there—apart from Ross Dawson, of course, and the idiotic pipedream her father seemed to have that if she and Ross Dawson became one, Edward Bradbury might one day rule a Bradbury, Dawson and Cross empire.

No chance. Ross had spoken of her 'mythical husband.' Quite when she had let it generally be known that she was married she wasn't sure.

Probably around the same time as she had discovered the extent of her father's unscrupulous behaviour.

Probably around the same time her backbone had started to stiffen. Prior to that, having learned a passive 'anything for a quiet life' manner from her mother, she would never have dreamed of going against her father's wishes. Though, on thinking about it, perhaps Nathan standing up to him had been the wake-up call she had needed.

Realising she was in danger of drifting off again, Phelix renewed her concentration on what the speaker was saying. 'Face-to-face meetings are better than a video link,' he was opining. What that had to do with their businesses she hadn't a clue, and knew she was going to have to pay closer attention. Though in her view it was still farcical that she was there at all.

With quite a long break for lunch, Phelix took herself off back to her hotel. Her father had wanted her to 'network' so he said. Tough! That was a lie, anyway.

Up in her room, she went to open her laptop. But, feeling mutinous all of a sudden, she ignored it. She didn't feel like working. She took some fruit and the cellophane wrapped slice of cake from the platter residing on a low table, added the chocolate that had been placed on her pillow when her bed had been turned down last night, went out to the balcony and stretched out on the sun-lounger.

The scenery was utterly fantastic. In the foreground a

church—complete with clockface to remind her that she had to attend the conference centre that afternoon—and behind, towering, majestic mountains. Forests of pine trees right and left. Tall… Somehow she found she was thinking of tall, towering Nathan Mallory—and this time she let her thoughts go where they would.

They had married, she and Nathan, on a warm, humid day. She had worn what she had thought then, but blushed about now, to be a smart blue two piece. She supposed she must have worried a bit, after she had bought it because it had fitted her then. But on her wedding day, it had literally hung on her. Nathan—a stern-faced Nathan—had worn a smart suit for the occasion.

Because he'd been waiting for an extremely important business telephone call her father had been unable to attend, but had said he would be home when they got there. And that had annoyed Nathan because it had meant he would have to go back with her to her home to exchange their marriage certificate for the cheque that would save Mallory and Mallory from losing everything.

'I'm s-sorry,' she'd stammered, half believing from Nathan's tough look that he would change his mind about going through with it.

But apart from muttering, 'What sort of a father is he?' Nathan had kept to his part of the bargain—even to the extent of holding her hand as they came away from the register office.

'Is that it?' she'd asked nervously.

'That's it,' he had confirmed. 'I expect there'll be a few more formalities to deal with to undo the knot…'

But the knot had never been undone. It should have been. They had originally planned it should be so. But, as matters had turned out, their marriage had never been annulled.

'Where did you leave your car?' Nathan had asked.

'I—um—don't drive,' she'd answered, newly married and starting to dislike the wimp of a creature she, through force of circumstance, had become. As soon as she had that ten percent she was going to have driving lessons, despite what her father said. She would buy a car…

'We'll go in mine,' Nathan had clipped, and had escorted her to the car park.

Her home was large, imposing and, despite Grace Roberts' attempts to brighten it up with a few flowers, cheerless. Grace had had no idea that the daughter of the house had that day married the handsome man by her side, and had been her usual pleasant self to Phelix.

'Your father had to go out urgently,' she said. 'But he left a message for you to leave the document in his study and said he'll attend to it.'

Hot, embarrassed colour flared to Phelix's face, a horrible dread starting to take her that her father might be intending to renege on the part of the deal he had made with Nathan Mallory. That Nathan, his competitor, having kept his part of the bargain, had been hung out to dry!

'Thank you, Grace,' she managed. 'Er—this is Mr Mallory…er…'

'Shall I get you some tea?' Grace asked, seeming to realise she was struggling.

'That would be nice,' Phelix answered and, as Grace went kitchenwards, 'My father must have left an envelope for you in his study,' Phelix suggested. Hoping against hope that her fears were groundless, and that there would be an envelope on the desk with Nathan's name on it, she led the way to the study.

But there was no envelope. Scarlet colour scorched her cheeks again, and she felt she would die of the humiliation of it. 'I'm s-sorry,' she whispered to the suddenly cold-eyed man by her side. 'I'm sure my father will be home soon,' she went on, more in hope than belief. 'Shall we have tea while we wait?'

Apart from Henry Scott, who had occasionally in the past called at the house with important papers for her father to sign,

Phelix was unused to entertaining anyone. If her father had been delayed, her mother had always offered Henry refreshment of some kind.

So copying her mother's graceful ways, even if she was feeling awkward, Phelix gave her new and promised to be temporary husband tea.

It was Grace Roberts' evening off—she was going to the theatre and would be staying with a friend overnight. 'You've everything you need?' she enquired, with a professional look around.

'Everything's fine, thank you, Grace. Enjoy the theatre,' Phelix bade her.

'Grace has been with you for some while?' Nathan, with better manners than her father, stayed civilly polite to ask a question he could have no particular interest in knowing the answer to.

'About six years—she adored my mother.'

'Your mother died recently in a road accident, I believe?'

Phelix did not want to talk about it. Never would she forget the horror of that night. The day had been a day similar to today. Warm, sticky, and with thunder in the air.

'I'm truly very sorry,' she said abruptly. 'I can't think what's keeping my father.' And, feeling sure that Nathan did not want to spend a minute longer with her than he had to, 'Look, if you've somewhere you've got to be, I can give you a ring the moment my father comes in.'

Nathan Mallory stared at her long and hard then, and she could not help but wonder if he suspected she was giving him the same run-around that her father seemed to be giving him.

But, deciding to give her the benefit of the doubt, 'I'll wait,' he clipped. 'That cheque is my last remaining option.'

And Phelix knew then from the set of this man's jaw that, in order to save his firm for him and his father, Nathan Mallory was having to bite on a very unpleasant bullet. Having completed his side of the bargain, he now had to wait for the man who had offered him the deal to complete his part. Yet Phelix just knew, as she looked numbly into Nathan Mallory's stern grey eyes, that everything in him was urging him to leave. That if there was any other way he would have taken it. *She* felt humiliated, but that must be nothing to what this proud man must be feeling. And yet for his business, for his father, it was, as he said, his last remaining option.

'D-does your father know about today?' she asked tentatively.

'I thought I'd prefer to have that cheque in my hand before I told him.'

That made her feel worse. 'I'm sorry,' she said quietly. 'I truly am.'

He looked at her again, and his expression softened slightly. 'I know,' he replied.

And the next two hours had ticked by with still no sign of her father.

'Will you excuse me?' she said at one point, and went to her father's study to make a call to her father's PA. But Anna Fry said she had no idea where he was. 'Is Mr Scott free?' Phelix asked. And, when she was put through, 'Henry? Phelix. Do you know where my father is? I need to contact him rather urgently.'

Henry did not know where he was either. But, alarmed at her anxious tone, he was ready to come over at once to help with her problem, whatever it was. Phelix thanked him, but said it was nothing that important.

So she went back to Nathan, gave him the evening paper to read—and started to grow anxious on another front. The sky had darkened to almost black when she heard the first rumble of thunder. Thunderstorms and their violence terrified her.

She tried to think of something else, but at the first fork of lightning she was again reliving that night—the night her mother had died. There had been one horrendous storm that night. She had been in bed asleep when the first crack of thunder had awakened her. She had sat up in bed, half expecting that her mother would come and keep her company—her mother did not like storms either.

It was with that in mind that as the storm had become more fearsome, Phelix had shot along to her mother's room to check that she was all right. Only as she had quickly opened the door a fork of lightning, swiftly followed by another, had lit up her mother's room—and the scene that had met her eyes had sent her reeling. Phelix had plainly seen that her mother was not alone in her bed. Edward Bradbury was there too.

'What are you doing?' Phelix had screamed—he was *assaulting* her mother!

Her father had bellowed at her to leave in very explicit, crude language. But at least her interruption had had the effect of taking his attention briefly away from her mother, and her mother had been able to dive from the bed and pull a robe around her shoulders.

'Go back to bed, darling,' she'd urged.

Phelix had not known then which terrified her the more: the violent storm or the dreadful scene she had happened across which was now indelibly imprinted on her mind for evermore.

But there was no way she was going to leave. 'No, I'll—' But she had been urged from the room.

'We'll talk about it in the morning,' her mother had promised, and pushed her to the other side of the door. They had been the last words she had ever said to her. By morning she'd been dead.

A fork of lightning jerked her to awareness that she was in her father's drawing room with the man she had that day married. It looked as if it was going to be another of those horrendous storms. Rain was furiously lashing at the windows, and as another fork of lightning speared the room Phelix only just managed to hold back from crying out.

'W-would you mind very much if I left you to wait by yourself?' she asked, feeling that at any moment now she would disgrace herself by either shouting out in panic or bolting from him.

'Not at all,' Nathan replied and, realising he would probably quite welcome his own company, she fled.

Hoping she could get into bed, hide her head under the bedclothes and wait for morning, when her father would have paid Nathan the money he'd promised, Phelix quickly undressed. No way, with that storm raging, was she going to take her usual shower.

She got into bed, but left her bedside lamp on. She did not want to lie in the dark, when she would again see that ugly scene in her mother's bedroom that night. Phelix closed her eyes and tried to get some rest. It was impossible.

She had no idea what time it was when, wide awake, she heard the storm which she had hoped had begun to fade return with even greater ferocity. It seemed to be directly overheard when there was a violent crack of thunder like no other—and then the lights went out.

Only vicious forks of lightning, in which she again saw her father's evil face, her mother's pleading, illuminated her bedroom. Striving desperately to banish the images tormenting her mind, Phelix made herself remember that she might still have a guest—a husband she had abandoned to his own devices.

Pinning her thoughts on Nathan, who had already been dealt a raw deal by her father and who might now be sitting in the drawing room in the dark, Phelix left her room and raced down the stairs. 'Nathan!' she called, her voice somewhere between a cry and a scream as thunder again cracked viciously directly overhead.

In the light of another fork of lightning she saw he was still there, had heard her, had come from the drawing room and had seen her.

'You all right?' he asked gruffly.

Words failed her. The fact that he was still there showed how very badly he needed that money. 'Oh, Nathan,' she whispered miserably, and in a couple of strides he was over to her, his hands on her arms.

'Scared?' he asked gently.

'T-terrified.' She was too upset to dissemble.

Nathan placed a soothing arm about her shoulders. 'You're shaking,' he murmured.

'It was a night like this when my mother was killed,' she replied witlessly.

'Poor love,' he murmured, and she had never known that a man could be so kind, so gentle. 'Come on, let's get you back to bed,' he said.

And, when she was too frozen by the empathy of the moment to be able to move, he did no more than pick her nightdress-clad body up in his arms and carry her up the winding staircase, his way lit by fork after fork of blinding lightning.

Phelix had left her bedroom door open in her rush, and Nathan carried her in and placed her gently under the covers of her bed.

'Don't leave me!' she pleaded urgently as another cannon-shot of thunder rent the air.

She was immediately ashamed, but not sufficiently so to be able to tell him she would be all right alone, and, after a moment of hesitation, Nathan did away with his shoes, shrugged out of his suit jacket and came to lie on top of her bed beside her. It was a three quarter size bed, but for all she was five feet nine tall there was not much of her.

'Nothing can harm you,' he told her quietly, and in the darkness reached for her hand.

She had gone down the stairs with some vague notion that he would feel uncomfortable sitting alone in a strange house in the dark. But here he was comforting her!

Again she felt ashamed. Then lightning lit the room, and she was again in that nightmare of unwanted visions of that night in her mother's bedroom not so long ago. She clutched on to Nathan's hand.

'Shh, you're all right,' he soothed. 'It will be over soon.' And, maybe because her grip was threatening to break his fingers, he let go her hand and to her further comfort placed an arm around her thin shoulders. Instinctively she turned into him, burying her face in his chest.

Quite when, or how, she managed to drop off to sleep, she had no notion. But she was jerked awake when her bedside lamp suddenly came on—power restored.

'Oh!' she exclaimed, sitting up. 'Oh!' she exclaimed again. Nathan was still on the bed with her. He got to his feet and stood, unspeaking, looking at her. 'Oh, Nathan, I'm so sorry,' she apologised. The storm was over; normality was back.

He surveyed her troubled eyes, her blushing complexion—and more shame hit her. This man had married her—for nothing. He had trusted her father's word—for nothing. She wanted to cry, but managed to hold back her tears. This man, her husband, had suffered enough without him having to put up with her tears too.

'You didn't have dinner!' she gasped, suddenly appalled, although she could not have eaten a thing herself. But just then the headlights of a car coming up the drive flashed across the window. 'My father's home,' she offered jerkily, though was not taken aback when Nathan declined to rush out to meet him.

'I'm surprised he bothered,' he answered, bending to put on his shoes. But Phelix did not miss the hard note that had come to his voice.

'What will you do?' she asked, feeling crushed, sorrowfully knowing for certain now that her father did not intend to honour the deal he had made.

'Frankly, I honestly don't know,' Nathan answered tautly, and suddenly Phelix could not bear it.

'You can have my money,' she offered. 'I don't know yet how much it will be, but you can have it all. I'll—'

Nathan smiled then, a grim kind of a smile. 'Enough is enough,' he said.

'You—don't want it?'

Nathan shook his head. 'Not to put too fine a point on it, little one, I'd cut my throat before I'd touch a penny of Bradbury money,' he replied bluntly.

That 'little one' saved his remark from being as wounding as it would otherwise have been—and then they both heard the sound that told them that her father was coming up the stairs.

With the light of battle in his eyes, Nathan grabbed up his jacket and went out to confront him. Phelix hated rows, confrontation, but it started the moment her father saw Nathan coming from her bedroom.

'What the hell game do you think you're playing?' Edward Bradbury roared.

'I might well ask you the same question!'

'I checked—you married her.' There was a satisfied note in her father's voice.

'I kept my side of the bargain,' Nathan agreed coldly.

'Hard luck!'

'You're saying that you never had any intention of handing over that cheque?'

'I thought you'd have twigged before now,' her father gloated—and that was when Phelix discovered she had more backbone than she had thought. Which made it impossible for her to sit there and listen to the way her father, so careless of her, was so blatantly pleased with himself. 'You can forget all about getting a cheque from me,' he crowed.

'Father!' Phelix rushed from her room and out to the landing, ashamed, disgusted, and never more embarrassed to have such a parent. 'You can't possibly—'

'Don't you *dare* tell me what I can and cannot do!' her father bellowed.

'But you owe—'

'I owe him nothing! He can forget about the money, and—'

'And you, sir,' Nathan cut across—furiously, 'can shove your money!' And somehow or other—perhaps in the thinking time during the long hours of his wait, perhaps with Phelix offering him the money she was due—Nathan seemed to sense now, when he hadn't seen it before, that there was more in this for Edward Bradbury than allowing his daughter to have her own money. 'And while you're about it,' he went on, his eyes glinting fury, 'you can forget about the annulment too!'

That stopped Edward Bradbury dead in his tracks. 'What are you saying?' he demanded, looking more shaken than at any time Phelix had ever known.

'Exactly what it sounds as if I'm saying!' Nathan Mallory stood up to him.

Phelix saw her father's glance dart slyly to her bedroom—and saw unadulterated fury sour his expression, none too sweet before. 'Is this true?' he turned to demand of his nightdress-clad daughter, his voice rising to a screaming roar when she was not quick enough to answer him. *'Is this true?'* Hot colour flared to her face. She might be naïve in certain areas, but she knew what he was asking. *'Is it?'* he shouted.

Her throat felt suddenly dry. She wasn't sure what was happening here, but by the sound of it—if she'd got it right—Nathan wanted to score off her father by letting him think they had been—lovers.

Colour flared to her face again. Even her ears felt hot. But just then she truly felt that, in the light of her father's conduct, she owed more loyalty to Nathan, the man she had married, than to her father.

'If you're asking have I slept with Nathan since our marriage, Father, then the answer is yes. Yes, I have,' she answered. She did not dare look at Nathan as she said it, but realised full well what the huge lie implied—just as she realised that she must have said the right thing.

Because without a word to her Nathan, his chin jutting, leaned to her father, told him to, 'Put that in your dishonourable drum and bang it, Bradbury,' and walked down the stairs and out of the house.

And that was the last time she had seen him. Though even with her father's plan for the marriage annulment scuppered it had not prevented Edward Bradbury from searching for an alternative route to get the marriage annulled. He'd still been nefariously plotting when, a few days later, Phelix had discovered exactly why that annulment was so important to him.

Feeling sickened that her own flesh and blood could care so little for her that he could so deliberately attempt to cheat her, Phelix had lost what little respect she'd had for her father. For the first time ever she had dug her heels in and refused to listen to any further talk of an annulment, or for that matter a divorce.

Had Nathan wanted a divorce or an annulment she would have agreed at any time. But he had not made any representation to that effect.

The church clock in front of her chiming the quarter hour brought Phelix back to the present.

Knowing she had to get back to the conference, she jumped up from the sun lounger, her thoughts promptly shooting back to Nathan Mallory. The night of their wedding was the last time she had seen him or had had any contact with him until today. She remembered his gentleness, his arm about her…

Stop it! She made her way to the conference knowing she was going to have to stop drifting off to relive matters that had taken place so long ago. She supposed it was just seeing Nathan again so unexpectedly that had set her off.

It was for sure she would have given Davos a very wide berth had she thought for a moment that he would be here this week. She had been aware, of course, that Mallory and Mallory had long since pulled themselves out of the financial crater they had been in. They were now one of the most top-notch companies in the business. But she had been certain that the heads of such large companies would not be bothered with this week's conference, but would be circling around from next week, when the big noises from JEPC Holdings would be leading the show.

And yet, as she entered the conference centre, did it matter that Nathan Mallory was here? He had said hello and that was the end of it.

Nevertheless, as she spotted Duncan and Chris and made her way over to them, she could not help but be glad that, although still slender, she had filled out a little, had curves in the right places, and had developed a sense of style that suited her.

She took her seat and noticed Nathan Mallory seated some way away. She had done nothing either about an annulment or a divorce from him. And since she had not received any papers to sign from him, she could only assume that—although he was now more than financially able to support a wife—there could not be anyone in particular in his life.

After striving to concentrate on what the present speaker was talking about—'Strategy and Vision'—she was glad when they broke for refreshments. She told Chris she was going outside for some air, and made haste before Ross Dawson should waylay her.

It was a beautiful day, sunny and too lovely to be stuck indoors. She strolled out into the adjacent park and felt as near content as at any time in her life. She ambled on, in no hurry, pausing to bend and read the inscription on a monument in tribute to Sir Arthur Conan Doyle, who had apparently brought the new sport of skiing to the attention of the world by skiing over the mountain from Davos to Arosa.

No mean feat, she was thinking, when a well remembered voice at the back of her asked, 'Enjoying your freedom?'

She straightened, but knew who it was before she turned around and found herself looking up—straight into the cool grey eyes of Nathan Mallory. 'I didn't know you'd be here!' she exclaimed without thinking.

'Otherwise you'd have kept away?'

Phelix hesitated, then knew that she did not want Nathan to form an impression that she was as dishonest as her father. It took an effort, but she managed to get herself back together. 'I still feel dreadful when I think of our last meeting.' She did not avoid his question. She knew he would never forget their wedding day and its outcome either. 'You've done so well since then,' she hurried on.

He could have said that it was no thanks to the Bradburys, but by dint of sheer night-and-day labour he and his father had managed to turn their nose-diving company around and into the huge thriving concern that it was today. What he did say was, 'You haven't done so badly either, from what I hear.' He did not comment on the physical change in her, but it was there in his eyes. 'Shall we stretch our legs?' he suggested.

She felt nervous of him suddenly. But he had never done her the least harm; the reverse, if anything. She remembered the way he had stayed with her that awful storm-ridden night when she had been so terrified.

It was not an overly large park, and as she stepped away from the monument Nathan matched his step to hers and they strolled the kind of a horseshoe-shaped path.

'You heard I studied law?' she asked, feeling in the need to say something.

'I'm acquainted with Henry Scott,' Nathan replied. 'I bump into him from time to time at various business or fundraising functions. I knew he worked at Bradburys, and asked him once if he knew how you were getting on. He's very fond of you.'

'Henry's a darling. I doubt I'd have got through my exams without his help.'

'From what he said, I'm sure you would.' Nathan looked down at her. 'You've changed,' he remarked.

She knew it was for the better. 'I needed to! When I look back—'

'Don't,' Nathan cut in. 'Never look back.'

She shrugged. 'You're right, of course.'

'So tell me about this new Phelix Bradbury.'

'There's not a lot to tell,' she replied. 'I worked hard—and here I am.'

'And that covers the last eight years?' he queried sceptically.

He halted, and she halted with him, and all at once they were facing each other, looking into each other's eyes. Her heart suddenly started to go all fluttery, so that she had to turn from him to get herself together. She supposed she had always known that this, 'the day of reckoning,' would come.

She took a deep breath as she recognised that day was here. 'What you're really asking,' she began as they started to stroll on again, 'is what was the real reason my father wanted me married *and* single again with all speed?' She was amazed that, when she was feeling all sort of disturbed inside somehow, her voice should come out sounding so even.

'It would be a good place to begin,' Nathan murmured.

He was owed. Owed more than that she just tell him about herself. And he, she realised, wanted the lot. 'I'm sure you've guessed most of it,' she commented. She glanced over to him, and caught the slight nod of his head.

'I was too desperate in my need to save the company to look for hidden angles in your father's offer. But as I started to take on board that I'd been had, I began to probe deeper. And, while I still didn't know "what", it didn't take a genius to realise—too late,' he inserted, 'that there had to be some other reason why your father wanted you in and out of a marriage in five minutes.'

That 'too late' made her wince. But she was honest enough to know that it was justified. 'You were quicker at picking that up than me,' she remarked, remembering how it had been that night. 'That's why you let my father believe an—er—annulment was out of the question, wasn't it?'

'It was the first time I'd seen him with you. It was pretty

obvious from the way he spoke of and to you that an annulment was more important to him than simply doing a father's duty and watching out for you. His prime concern, clearly, was that annulment.' Nathan shrugged. 'As enraged as I was, the question just begged to be asked—if he was so uncaring, why was he going to such extraordinary lengths to help his daughter gain ten percent of her inheritance.'

'You knew that there must be some other reason?'

'By then every last scrap of my trust in the man had gone. It didn't take long for me to see that, shark that he is, there had to be something in it for him.'

It should, she supposed, have upset her to hear her father referred to as a shark, but what Nathan Mallory was saying was no more than the truth. My word, was he telling the truth! 'There was,' she had to agree. Now that she was in possession of the true facts of her grandfather's will, she was totally unable to defend her father. And since the man she had married had been the one to have suffered most, she did not see how—or why for that matter—she should try to defend her father's atrocious actions either. 'There was something in it for him,' she confessed quietly. 'Something he had no chance to claim should I stay married.'

Nathan looked down at her as they ambled along. 'You're not going to leave it there, I hope?' he enquired evenly.

For a few seconds Phelix struggled with a sense of disloyalty to her father. But he had long since forfeited any right to her loyalty. And Nathan *was owed*! 'My father had plans that would never come to fruition if that annulment did not take place,' she said at last. 'But you'd realised that, hadn't you?'

'Sensed, more than knew,' Nathan replied, but asked sharply, 'Did you know in advance—?'

'No!' she protested hotly, not wanting to be tarred by the same disreputable brush as her father. 'I didn't so much as suspect...I'd not the smallest idea. I was still totally in the dark

the next morning, when Henry Scott came to the house with some paperwork he needed to go through with my father. When my father was hung up with some business on the phone, I made Henry some coffee. Grace, our housekeeper, wasn't back,' Phelix vividly recalled.

'She'd had the previous night off—she'd been to the theatre.'

'You remember that!'

'I have forgotten absolutely nothing about that night!' Nathan said grimly.

Her heart did a peculiar kind of flutter. She had lain in her bed. He had cradled her close. 'Er—Grace is still with us. She should have retired ages ago, but... Anyway.' Phelix strove to get back to what they were saying, and came abruptly down to earth when close on that memory she thought of her father returning home that night. 'I was a bit down—still coming to terms with my mother's sudden death, and— Well, anyway, Henry—with the patience of a saint, I have to say—dragged from me what had happened.'

'You told him you'd got married?' Nathan's tone had sharpened.

'There's no need to sound so tough! I was very upset over the way you had been treated! I told him my father had defaulted on some money he'd promised a businessman—er—who was down on his luck—to marry me. But I never said who the man was, and I never would. Nor, you can be sure, would my father.'

Nathan nodded. 'So you told Henry Scott that you'd married, and why?' he prompted.

'And I'm glad I did,' she answered. 'Henry's got a shrewder head than me. He asked if I'd seen my grandfather's will. I hadn't, of course. So Henry then asked me what the letter from my grandfather's solicitors had said.'

'But you hadn't received any letter from them,' Nathan stated.

'You're shrewder than me too,' she commented.

'You were standing too close to the picture to see it as Henry Scott and I see it.'

'I suppose you're right. Anyhow—' she broke off. 'I must be boring you with all of this.'

'Don't you dare stop now,' Nathan ordered. 'I've waited eight years to hear this!'

Phelix flicked him a sharp look. Oh, my, was he owed! 'I'm—er—trying not to be too disloyal to my father here...' she began—and had her ears scorched for her trouble.

'Good God, woman!' Nathan snarled fiercely, halting in his stride. 'You think that man deserves your loyalty?' Phelix stopped walking too and looked up into Nathan's angry grey eyes. 'For his own ends—whatever they were—he *used* you! In doing so he thereby gave up all right to any loyalty from you!' But suddenly then Nathan seemed to pause in his anger, somehow seeming to collect himself, and he was much less angry when, quietly, he promised, 'You have my word, Phelix, that whatever it was your father was up to I won't broadcast it.'

Phelix looked from him. Never would she ever have thought the day would come when she would stroll in a park with a man she barely knew, even if admittedly she was married to him, and reveal the full extent of her father's treachery. But, as Nathan had intimated, some sort of an explanation was eight years overdue.

But here she was hesitating. Yet had not her father been instrumental in trying to ruin Nathan? Because by going back on his word about the money that was what could have happened. Perhaps Nathan was fully entitled to know the real reason behind that marriage deal.

'Anyway...' She took a steadying breath, started to walk on, and, as Nathan suited his steps to hers, she plunged. 'Henry—who seems to know just about everybody—telephoned me when he got back to his office and told me he had made an appointment for me with my grandfather's legal people.'

'You didn't tell your father?'

She shook her head. 'I think it was about then that I started to grow up.' She took another steadying breath, and relived the shock of what she had learned when she had kept that appointment. 'Anyhow, the lawyers were quite astounded, and couldn't understand why I hadn't received any of their letters.' It had all become clear to her then why her father had suddenly started spending his mornings working from home—he had wanted to be there when the post arrived. 'But I was as astonished as they had been that their correspondence had gone astray when they read that Grandfather Bradbury, a man who'd had a thing about divorce, had left me money conditionally. As my father had told me, should I marry before I was twenty-five I was to receive ten percent of the whole cash sum. But—and this is what I did not know—should that marriage fail, either by annulment or divorce, before I reached twenty-five, then the remainder of the money and a considerable portfolio of shares, including thousands of shares in Edward Bradbury Systems, were to go with immediate effect to my father.'

'My God! The man's a—' Nathan broke off. 'So that was what he was after—your shares! An annulment would have given them to him straight away.'

'An annulment is fairly instant. To divorce, a couple have to be married for more than a year.'

'And your father did not want to wait that long to get his hands on those shares?'

'He did not,' she had to agree. And, having come to the end, with everything said that Nathan had waited long enough to hear, she turned to him. 'That's it, I'm afraid. The whole sorry tale.'

Looking at him, she saw with surprise a hint of a smile come to the corners of his mouth. 'So how do you feel now about having snookered his plans?'

Her lips twitched. She had to smile too. She had aided and abetted Nathan by going along with his hint that an annulment had been forfeited. 'In all truth, I *had* slept with you,' she murmured lightly.

'Tut-tut,' Nathan scolded. 'My memory's better than that.'

She could feel her cheeks growing warm. She hadn't blushed in years. Time to change the subject.

'I know he's my father, but he didn't deserve any less.' The subject was done with, the explanation Nathan was owed made—the least he was owed and, 'What do you think of the conference so—?' she began lightly.

'You're wearing a wedding ring!' Nathan abruptly cut in.

'That's probably because I'm married.'

'You're living with someone?' he demanded sharply.

She shook her head and just had to laugh. 'Now run for the hills!'

Nathan stared at her, seemed to like the sound of her laughter. 'I hope I'm braver than that,' he murmured. 'I'll prove it,' he added. 'I'll take you to dinner.'

Somehow—perhaps because she was a little on edge from having revealed the unpleasantness of what she'd had to reveal, or perhaps because she had been her own person for so long now—it niggled her a little that instead of asking he should just assume he would take her to dinner and that was all there was to it.

'I'm sorry,' she stated politely. 'I've arranged to have dinner with someone else.'

They had halted again, and Nathan held her glance for long moments. And then slowly he drawled, 'Don't I, as a mere husband, get priority?'

Her heart seemed to give a giddy kind of flip at Nathan claiming to be her husband. But somehow she managed to appear outwardly cool. 'I can't imagine you being a "mere" anything,' she answered. And all at once they were both grinning—and suddenly she was falling a little in love with him all over again.

CHAPTER THREE

THIS would never do, Phelix berated herself as she dressed to have dinner with Ross that night. All she seemed to think about was Nathan Mallory. It just would not do.

Had she been too friendly with him? How else should she have been? She should, she felt, be feeling a little disloyal to her father, but strangely she wasn't. She concentrated her thoughts on her father.

It had been a tremendous shock when the lawyers had told her the full contents of her grandfather's will, she recalled. Shaken rigid still did not cover how she had felt! She had been rocked, utterly amazed as the extent of her father's treachery had sunk in. Had that annulment taken place she would have lost everything bar that ten percent of actual cash willed to her. Her father would have grabbed everything else from her. Not by accident, but by evil, scheming design.

Only then had she started to realise why he had objected to her wanting to marry Lee Thompson. Had she married Lee she would have lived with him as his wife, with an annulment out of the question. Even should that marriage have ultimately ended in divorce it would have taken too long. Apart from the fact her father could not have hoped to hide the contents of her grandfather's will for as long as a year, he had not wanted to wait a moment longer than he had to to claim her shares.

And she had known nothing of what he had planned! But Nathan, without a clue as to what her father had been up to, had been far more aware than her. He must have started to work out that there was something rotten going on while he'd waited all those long hours for her father to return home.

There had been no annulment anyway, and, since Nathan was long overdue some kind of an explanation, she was glad she had today told him what she had.

Deciding to drive to Ross Dawson's hotel, Phelix went to collect her hired car reflecting that the marriage was neither annulled nor, when at any time after they had been married a year, Nathan could have applied for a divorce, had he done so.

'As stunning as ever!' Ross exclaimed the moment he saw her.

She smiled. 'You're so good for my ego.'

'I speak only the truth,' he replied, and escorted her into the dining room.

Phelix had always found him straightforward and uncomplicated, and to a certain extent felt relaxed in his company. He was one of the few men she dated, and even so he had known from the outset that she was married, and that nothing was ever going to come from her agreeing to have the occasional dinner with him.

That did not prevent him from trying, however. 'Does your husband know where you are tonight?' he asked as they consulted their menus. He was forever trying to fish for information on the man he more often than not called her 'mythical husband.'

But tonight, instead of side-stepping his question or fobbing him off with some kind of non-answer, she replied, 'As a matter of fact,' she replied, and was pleased to be able to answer without prevarication for once, 'he does. That is, he knows I'm in Davos.'

'He does?' Ross looked a touch taken aback.

'He does,' she confirmed.

'But you're still living with your father? You don't live with this phantom husband?'

'He travels a lot.' She knew for a fact he had journeyed to Switzerland.

'He's not in England either at the moment?' Ross pressed.

'He's abroad.'

'Where?'

Phelix was starting to wish that she had opted for a non-answer. 'Do you really need to know?' she asked.

'I'd like to meet him.'

'Why?'

'Because I'd like to tell him to give you a divorce—so you can marry me.'

At which point Phelix just had to burst out laughing. And in doing so she glanced up—straight into the icy cold eyes of Nathan Mallory, the very man under discussion.

He and his female companion had obviously just come into the dining room. Phelix would have offered a friendly kind of hello, but the word, along with the laughter on her lips, froze when with the barest inclination of his head in acknowledgement that he had seen her, Nathan walked straight by her.

'Will you?'

With her heartbeats playing double time, Phelix jerked her attention back to Ross Dawson, who had not noticed the tall couple pass behind him. 'Will I what?' she queried absently. She was feeling hurt by Nathan Mallory's cool attitude—nor did she care too much that he had the tall blonde in tow.

'I've just asked you to marry me.'

'You said you wouldn't!' Already Phelix was denying that she cared a scrap that the cold, unfriendly brute had so soon changed from the friendly man she had strolled in the park with that afternoon. Nor, when he had stated he would take *her* to dinner that evening, that it had not taken him very long to tell some other female that she had been elected.

'Are you really married?' Ross was asking.

And Phelix heaved a heavy sigh. 'I'm sharing a meal with

you, Ross, because I like you. My marriage,' she went on, and meant it, 'is not up for discussion.'

Ross sighed too. 'You're saying I'm to either accept that or dine alone?'

Put like that it sounded a bit blunt, but… 'That's what it amounts to, Ross. I'm sorry.'

'Your old man would like us to get together,' he tried.

That seemed to her to be one very good reason not to. But, while it had not seemed so tremendously disloyal to discuss her father with Nathan, there was no one else apart from Henry to whom she would allow that privilege.

She attempted to change the subject. 'What do you think of the conference so far?'

'I do love you, you know.'

'Then eat your spinach—and behave yourself.'

He laughed, and she knew she was more fond of him than just liking. But as he complained, 'Chance to do anything other than behave myself with you would be a fine thing,' she knew that love him she did not.

More than a dozen times as their meal progressed Phelix felt the pull to look over in the direction of where she knew Nathan and the blonde were sitting. But somehow, and it was not easy, she managed to keep her eyes from straying in that direction.

But she was glad when the meal was over. Though when she and Ross were ready to leave the dining room she was still concentrating on not looking to where Nathan was. He thought, after the friendly way they had been with each other that afternoon, that he could just more or less ignore her? Okay, so he had inclined his head a touch, but a friendly hello wouldn't have hurt him.

Realising she was making too much of what she was letting herself believe was a snub, Phelix was glad she had some superb clothes. The green, just above the knee, dress she was wearing was one such article. Poised, generally aloof, but smiling at her dinner partner, she walked from the dining room with Ross Dawson staking his claim by placing a guiding arm lightly across her back. She had shrugged his arm away from her the last time he had done that, and did so again—but not until they were out of sight of the dining room.

'Something to drink to finish off with?' Ross asked.

'Better not.'

'You can't be going back to work!'

'Why not?' enquired she who had not opened her laptop since she had got there!

'I'll walk you back,' Ross offered.

'I drove here.'

'One of these days…' he promised.

'Goodnight, Ross.' She smiled, but found he was still escorting her to where she had parked her car.

He kissed her on both cheeks, gripped her arms as though he would like to pull her to him, but decided, in the hope of seeing her again soon, against it. They bade each other a smiling farewell.

But Phelix was not smiling as she let herself into her hotel room. How dared he more or less ignore her? Who did Nathan Mallory think he was? Just because he was dining with that luscious blonde!

For a further five minutes, totally unused to men treating her that way, Phelix railed against him. But it was when she found herself thinking that for two pins she'd divorce the swine that her sense of humour surfaced—and she just had to laugh at herself.

They had been married for eight years—and never a cross word. And in truth, no matter how cranky he was, she did not want to divorce him. Perhaps, once this conference was over, it would be another eight years of complete harmony before she saw him again.

Phelix showered and brushed her teeth, but when she climbed into bed she was starting to realise that if she was to be brutally honest she would *not* like another eight years to pass with never a sight of Nathan.

It was during her early-morning swim the next morning that she recalled her last waking thought before sleep had claimed her. But she was then able to dismiss it as nothing but a load of tosh.

She was still telling herself that she wouldn't give a button if she never saw him again when, making her way to breakfast, she bumped straight into him! As she stepped out of the lift he was coming from the direction of the breakfast dining room.

'Phelix,' he acknowledged her, covering his surprise better than she thought she covered hers that, by the look of it, they had opted to stay at the same hotel.

'Nathan.' She nodded, and did a smart, head in the air left turn away from him.

She was feeling all shaky inside when she sat down at her table. But for his surprise at seeing her there would he have spoken at all? she wondered. And was he staying here or had it been more a temporary stop-over—with the blonde?

Deciding that she did not want to know, Phelix suddenly discovered that she was not very hungry. Her small amount of cereal and coffee did not take long to consume, but she all at once felt hesitant to leave the room. What if…?

Phelix immediately took herself in hand. Heavens above, was she worried that she might bump into Nathan again? How ridiculous was that!

She did not see him in the hotel when, cross with herself, she left the breakfast room. Nor did she see him again when she made her way to the conference centre. But she did see him again, in the same seat he had occupied yesterday. She was more aware of him than she was the present speaker. But then, that speaker having come to an end and been applauded, she watched as Nathan Mallory, having stepped into the breach for the person who had been scheduled to speak, left his seat to address the assembled audience.

For no known reason she felt all churned up inside, but started to relax as Nathan began, quite obviously at ease with his subject. Most peculiarly, when apart from that slip of paper—their marriage certificate—he was nothing to do with her, her heart filled with pride. She watched him with riveted attention as he spoke clearly, concisely and confidently. Then all at once he seemed to look directly at her and—hesitate. But it was only for the briefest moment before he was going smoothly on again.

When he came to an end he received well-earned applause—and Phelix was at one and the same time proud and choked. She felt a desperate need to be on her own, and was glad that at that moment there was a general break for refreshments.

'Coffee?' Duncan asked before she could make a bolt for it.

'I'll—er—get back to my hotel. I need to make some phone calls,' she replied, ready to invent anything in her need to be alone.

With other delegates congesting her way, her exit was not as speedy as she had hoped. But at last she was outside the conference centre and walking quickly along the Promenade—the main street—towards her hotel.

Oh, Nathan! He had been wonderful. Just looking at him…

No! Stop thinking about him! She did not know what it was about him, but he was having the strangest effect on her. She admired him tremendously. Why wouldn't she? There had not been a sound to be heard when he had been giving his speech.

That did not explain, though, why she had been feeling so mixed up inside about him that she had needed to get out of there.

Phelix suddenly became aware then that she had walked quite some way, and she began to slow her pace. She was not sure that she wanted to go back to her hotel.

But it was then that she saw that she was nearing the Schatzalp funicular that would take her a good way up the towering mountain. Davos was said to be the highest town in Switzerland. The funicular was just what she needed to carry her up and away. She needed to clear her head. Perhaps the pure air up there would help her do it.

Regardless that she should be taking her seat at the conference, Phelix executed a smart right turn and inside the next five minutes was seated in one of the compartments, waiting for the vehicle to start its climb.

But so much for her hoping to escape her mixed-up feelings! Because before the car could set off someone else had joined her compartment, and as shock hit her, and warm colour surged to her face, her emotions went chaotic. Stumped for anything to say, she just sat and stared at the tall dark-haired man who had just entered.

'Bunking off?' Nathan Mallory enquired equably.

Somehow, and from where she had no idea, Phelix managed to find a cool note. 'All work, etcetera,' she returned calmly as he took a seat on the bench next to her. She then sought feverishly for something else to say. 'Good speech, by the way,' she remarked lightly. And, as she realised that he had probably decided to go up the mountain to clear his head too, 'Er—if you want to be alone…' she began.

'Had I wanted to do that, I wouldn't have followed you from the conference,' he replied evenly.

'You followed me?' she asked in surprise as the vehicle started off. Last night he hadn't wanted to know her—this morning either for that matter. Yet now…? She opted to go for the impersonal route. 'It's no good talking to me about business. I'm on the legal side, so wouldn't know—'

'I've no interest in your family's business,' Nathan butted in, and seemed more interested in enjoying the ride than in enlightening her as to why he had followed her. Presumably he wanted to speak with her about something.

When they alighted from the vehicle some five or six minutes later, Nathan seemed content to wander around the kind of plateau a good way up the mountain that housed a café-restaurant and a small souvenir kiosk.

'Shall we have coffee?' Nathan asked, instead of telling her this time.

There was a large hotel further along, but it appeared to be closed, so they made their way to the café-restaurant, opting to have coffee outside, where they could take in the air while admiring the spectacular view.

Phelix had to admit that her emotions were still a little erratic, but she had not spent years outwardly being in control for nothing.

Nathan ordered their coffee, which arrived with a little heart-shaped biscuit. But if he had followed her for a reason, and it was not her family's business, she decided it must either be his business or—and oddly her heart gave a small lurch—personal.

But, apart from a few words of idle conversation, he seemed in no hurry to begin. And from her point of view, as she began to accept the moment and to just enjoy her splendid surroundings, she was in no hurry should he have decided to end their marriage. Although of course with the length of time they had lived apart, when he could have obtained a divorce at any time, there was absolutely no need for him to discuss it with her at all.

The view truly was breathtaking, and Phelix looked into the distance, watching brave hang-gliders soaring over the mountains that surrounded them. She did not want a divorce. It suited her very well to be married. But her family, or more precisely her father, had served Nathan with the sticky end, and if a divorce was what Nathan wanted, a divorce was what he would have.

Her attention was drawn to the nearby red-berried rowan trees to her left, and she found she was asking, 'Are you staying at the Schweizerhof?' and immediately wished that she hadn't. If he had been merely visiting, she didn't think she wanted to know.

'I thought my team might be more relaxed if I stayed elsewhere," he replied.

'There are three of you?' she queried, discovering she wanted to know his connection with the blonde, but trying to hide it.

'There were always meant to be three,' Nathan answered, not helping her at all.

'That would be you, substituting for your employee who couldn't make it, the other man, and...' she just could not hold back from asking, '...the blonde lady? Sorry,' Phelix apologised immediately. Grief, what was wrong with her? 'Perhaps the lady's more of a friend than...'

Nathan stared at her every bit as if he knew what she was thinking, and for a split second she hated him. 'Dulcie Green is a scientist,' he revealed. 'Brilliant in her field,' he added. 'We're very lucky to have her. But between you and me,' he murmured conspiratorially, 'I'd as soon have had dinner with my wife last night.'

Phelix laughed. Whether he was being serious or just plain charming, she had to laugh, though she guessed from his remark that he had taken Dulcie Green to dinner out of courtesy, when perhaps his other team member had been engaged elsewhere.

'How about you?' Nathan asked. 'You're not staying with Ward and Watson.'

It did not seem polite to mention that she would have been had her father had his way.

But before she could do more than shake her head. Nathan asked abruptly, 'Where's Dawson staying?'

She looked at him in surprise. 'What's Ross got to do with anything?'

He ignored her question. 'What is he to you?'

'What do you mean—what is he to me?'

'You know what I mean,' Nathan replied shortly.

From the way she remembered it—and she had known all along where Nathan's table was even if she had managed to keep her glance from straying—Ross had had his back to

Nathan. Though she supposed he could have caught a glimpse of Ross's face when they'd stood up to leave.

'Er.' She had no idea how to answer that statement.

'Does he know that you're married?'

Really, there was something of the terrier about Nathan Mallory, she decided! He wasn't leaving the subject of her relationship with Ross Dawson alone, anyway.

'He knows,' she replied. 'I'm not sure that he believes it—for all I tell him often enough—but he knows.'

'Do you intend to marry him?'

Phelix looked into Nathan's cool grey eyes, and away again. But, bearing in mind that Nathan had followed her, and must have done so for some reason, she thought she might ask a few questions of her own. 'I'm more than happy with the state of my present marriage, thank you. If you are?' she added, giving him an 'in' should he have followed her to tell her that in his view their marriage no longer served any useful purpose.

He did not take up the opening she had given him, and nor did he answer her question either, but asked instead, 'I take it from that that there's no one special?'

'Who has the time?' she lobbed back at him. But then she looked across to him and, observing the virile look of him, 'Well,' she qualified with a light laugh, 'you would. You'd make time. But…'

'But you've been busy getting on with your career?'

She shrugged her shoulders slightly. 'You must know how it is. You must have worked long hours—evenings, weekends too—to get where you wanted to be.'

'As did you,' he agreed, with a smile for her that just about melted her bones. 'So there's been no one special?'

She would have loved to ask him the same question, but changed her mind—she didn't think she wanted to know about the women in his life.

'No,' she replied—then suddenly remembered Lee Thompson.

'But?' Nathan queried, spotting her small moment of hesitation.

'There nearly was,' she said, but found that she didn't want to talk about anything unpleasant. 'I've finished my coffee. I think I'll make tracks.'

Nathan stood up with her and glanced about. 'We'll walk down,' he decided. She opened her mouth to protest; she just wasn't used to other people making such decisions for her. 'You've got the right shoes for it,' he added, his eyes on nowhere but her face, that alone telling her that he must have observed everything about her, right down to the flat heeled shoes she was wearing.

Her protest died unmade. She had just realised that she would like nothing better than to take the footpath down to Davos with him.

'Do you manage to get much exercise?' she asked, apropos of nothing, as they took the signposted Thomas Mann Weig to the zig-zagging mountain path.

'As much as I can. It's good to be outdoors. You?' he asked as, at a steady pace, they started on the walk that from a sign she had seen she calculated would take them forty or so minutes.

'We have a pool at home. I swim most mornings,' she replied, and enchantment started to wash over her as she paced with Nathan through the mountain pines, spotted the odd red squirrel shooting up them, and observed birds she did not know the name of flying by and settling in branches.

'You've had lovers, of course?' Nathan enquired after a while, quite unabashed at asking that which he wanted to know.

'We're still talking about exercise, I take it?' she enquired dryly.

He had the grace to grin, and her heart skipped a beat. 'No, actually,' he replied. 'Rather belatedly, I think I should just like to know more about this quite stunning woman I've been married to all this time.'

Her mouth fell open in surprise. Though she did not know which surprised her more, the fact that Nathan thought her stunning or the fact that he wanted to know more about her.

'Was that why you followed me, because…?' Had he really wanted to know more about her?

'Not solely because I want to know more of your love-life,' Nathan replied. 'Though I must admit I'm a shade intrigued that you wear a wedding ring.'

'You think I shouldn't?' she asked shortly.

'No need to get edgy,' he answered. 'Is it the same one I put there?' he asked.

'I never thought you'd mind. I mean, it's not as if anyone knows who I'm married to—'

'I don't mind,' he cut in.

'And it came in more than useful when I didn't want to date but needed to concentrate solely on my studies.'

Nathan took that on board. 'I bet it irritates the hell out of you father.'

'You could say that,' she replied lightly, recalling the thunderous row they'd had the first time had he noticed the ring on her finger. Though it had been more him bellowing and threatening and her standing firm for once and being determined not to take it off.

Nathan tried another tack. 'With or without that wedding ring, men are going to want to date you.'

'I've dated a few times,' she admitted, and was aware of Nathan's sharp glance at her. 'Nothing serious.'

'You're saying you've not had a lover?' Clearly he did not believe it. 'Dawson…?' he began.

'I'm not comfortable with this conversation.' She cut him off shortly. But immediately relented. She did not want to part bad friends. 'Not Ross, not anybody,' she added as they turned a bend in the path. But as Nathan abruptly halted, and she bumped into him, so in her too-speedy effort to take a pace away her foot slipped on a small collection of scree. But for Nathan catching hold of her, she would have fallen.

He held her close up to him, and suddenly her emotions were going haywire. 'No one?' he questioned. 'You've never…' Her mouth went dry—he was looking at her with a kind of warm look of surprise in his eyes.

'Absolutely never,' she murmured, and suddenly she just knew, as his glance went down to her parted lips, that he was going to kiss her.

But she was already shaken that he was so close, his hands on her arms still holding her to him, and she was not ready. She jerked away—and instantly wanted the moment back again. She wanted him to kiss her, wanted to feel that warm, wonderful mouth on hers. But too late now. She knew she would never again have the chance to feel his kiss.

Nathan made no attempt to hold on to her, but let her go and put some space between them as they carried on down the zig-zag path. And as Phelix began to get herself more of one piece again, she began to be certain that she had been totally wrong to imagine that Nathan had been about to kiss her; she could only blame that sudden heightened awareness of him that her emotions had gone off at a tangent.

They were walking side by side but with a fair space between them, and she was striving hard to concentrate on squirrels, birds, trees and pine cones—on anything but him—when, out of the blue, Nathan enquired, 'Do you have a hang-up about men, Phelix?'

That almost stopped her in her tracks. But she'd had years of experience in hiding her feelings, so she walked on and, in the same conversational tone he had used, 'Because I've never had a lover?' she asked.

'Not totally,' Nathan replied. 'You're twenty-six and are entitled to—have had experiences. But, at a guess, I'd say you had one fairly foul childhood. Your mother died tragically, and I doubt your father is the most sensitive of men.'

'You're psychoanalysing me?' she protested.

Nathan shook his head. 'What I am is feeling guilty that I never made contact with you in all this time to check that everything was going all right with your world.'

'You owe me nothing!' she exclaimed abruptly.

He was unabashed. 'I gave you my name. I should have done more.'

'Nonsense!' Phelix retorted sharply—and immediately regretted her sharp tone. She didn't know what was wrong with her, blowing first hot and then cold, annoyed one minute and then regretting it—she did not want to be bad friends with him. 'Anyhow, apart from the fact that you must have had one almighty row to hoe in those days of you and your father doing everything you could to turn your company around, you found out from Henry Scott how things were with me, what I was doing with my life.'

'Ah, yes, Henry,' Nathan murmured, but just then they came to the signposted junction where one road would lead in the direction of the conference centre, the other to Davos Platz and her hotel.

'I'm going this way,' Phelix said as they came to an amicable kind of halt.

'I'm committed to lunch with some people,' Nathan stated, and sounded as if he regretted that he had to go the other way. Charm, pure charm, she decided. 'I'd ask you to come along,' he added, 'but you work for the opposition.'

'I might have accepted—had I thought I was trusted,' she responded loftily.

But suddenly, as they stared into each other's eyes, they both started to smile. Her heart turned over.

'Want to come?' he invited after all.

And she felt all choked up suddenly. Oh, dear heaven! 'Better not,' she answered huskily from a suddenly constricted throat. But—before she could take her intended swift step away—Nathan just then took a step towards her.

'You are one very beautiful woman,' he said softly, and bent and kissed her cheek.

He took a step back, and she just had to let go a shaky breath. 'You're not so bad yourself,' she managed, and turned swiftly to the path she must take in fear that she might change her mind and ask if she could have lunch with him after all.

She walked away from him blindly, her mind in an uproar, her emotions in an uproar. Oh, how had it happened? Phelix swallowed, feeling devastated as a truth she could not deny hit her full force. She loved him! Heavens above—she loved Nathan Mallory!

Oh, help her, someone—she had fallen in love with Nathan. She was in love with him, Nathan, her husband—and any time now he could ask for a divorce!

CHAPTER FOUR

PHELIX was unseeing of anything as she made her way back to her hotel. She would have liked to have believed that what she felt for Nathan was mere infatuation. But it was not, and she knew that it was not. Oh, what had she done?

It had happened so quickly she could barely believe it, but it was there. Staggeringly, utterly staggeringly, it was there and would not go away. She was totally and completely in love with Nathan Mallory!

With her head in such a whirl, Phelix was back in her room before she had space to realise how very much Nathan must trust her. Had she gone with him to lunch he would have introduced her as Phelix Bradbury. That alone would have told the people he was lunching with who she was. Might even have jiggered up any deal he was making. It went without saying that her father, as hard-headed a businessman as they came, would—unless he'd had a complete personality change—have upset a few people in his day.

But she was more concerned with Nathan than with her father or any stuffy old business. How she had come to fall so hopelessly in love with Nathan she had no clue. Although it was true to say that she had always had a soft spot for him.

She recalled his gentleness with her eight years ago, when she had been something of a scared rabbit. She still loathed thunderstorms and knew, with those images of her father assaulting her mother still sharp in her mind, that she always would.

But Nathan, without knowing more than the bare bones that her mother had been killed during a storm, had held her and cradled her to sleep—so how could she not have a soft spot for him?

But this would never do. Realising that, apart from a small bowl of cereal at breakfast and that heart shaped biscuit at the café at Schatzalp, that she had eaten little that day, she left the hotel, found a café and had a snack, and then thought she had better make tracks for the conference. She had 'bunked off' that morning—she mustn't let the side down. Besides which, even if they never got to exchange so much as a word, she felt a great need to just see Nathan again.

She was in for a disappointment, however. She did not see him. What she thought of as his normal seat was empty, and stayed empty all afternoon. The blonde was there, and so was the other member of his team, but of Nathan Mallory she saw not a sign. And her heart began to ache.

And this, she started to know, was how it was going to be. And how could she bear it? She began to comprehend that now, with his speech over—the sole reason for him being there—and his lunch meeting over too, there was every chance that Nathan was on his way back to London.

'Are you going to have dinner with me tonight?' Ross Dawson caught up with her before she could leave the conference centre that afternoon.

Her appetite had disappeared again. As nice as Ross was, she wanted neither food nor his company. 'No can do,' she offered with an apologetic smile.

'You can't be working!' he protested. 'You're always working back home! But here—'

'I'll see you tomorrow, Ross,' she cut in firmly. She listened to a few more grumbles from him, and in order to escape—

when he saw that there was no changing her mind—she agreed to have lunch with him the next day.

It was still a glorious sunny afternoon, and back at her hotel Phelix went onto the balcony and from the sun-lounger tried to come to terms with what had happened to her, and her inability to do anything about it. She loved Nathan and he was on his way back to England; were it to be another eight years before she saw him again she did not know how she would bear it.

But her love for him was too new for her to focus on what she should do about it. Or how she must look forward to a future without him—a future where she would never see that smile, that wicked grin.

She felt cold suddenly, and realised that, for all the mountains were sunlit, the sun had gone over the top of the mountain nearest to her.

Leaving her lounger, she decided to kill some time by taking a shower. She wasn't hungry, but if she did feel peckish later she would order something from Room Service.

Nathan was in her head the whole time she was taking her shower; she was starting to realise the futility of attempting to push him out.

She was in the act of drying herself when there came an unexpected knock on her door. Thinking it might be one of the hotel staff, come to service the mini-bar or check up on something, Phelix swiftly donned the hotel's courtesy towelling robe and went to the door.

It was not a member of the hotel staff who stood there, however, but—to set her heartbeats drumming—none other than Nathan Mallory! 'I—er…' she gasped, a riot of emotions going on within her. Unspeaking, he stood silently looking at her. Her face was scrubbed clean of make-up, and as she sought for something fairly sensible to say, she knew her face was scarlet. 'I thought—thought you'd gone back to London,' she managed, albeit jerkily.

'Would I?' he replied laconically.

She was at a loss to know what to make of that for an answer. All she knew was that she was delighted to see him, and that he must want to see her, or why would he ask Reception for her room number?

'You're staying for the rest of the conference?' she asked, burbling on when it looked as if he *was* staying, 'I sort of thought, with your speech done, and the top brass not needing to be here until next Wednesday—' She broke off, amazed that the person she knew herself to be, that fairly reserved person, was babbling away like a nitwit. She compounded that thought when, suddenly aware that she was standing there in a robe that had come open at the top and which, from his height, must be giving Nathan a bird's-eye view of the top of her swelling creamy breasts, she exclaimed, 'I've got nothing on!' And there was Nathan's half smile again, and she loved him.

'I guessed,' he drawled, adding as he stretched out warm fingers and went to pull the edges of her robe together, 'With any other woman I might have construed that as an invitation.' A thrill shot up her spine as the backs of his fingers brushed briefly against the swell of her breasts. 'But knowing you, little Phelix, I'd say you're warning me that you're feeling a shade uneasy and wouldn't mind it I stated my business and left you to get dressed.'

Was she? She was too emotionally confused to know what she had meant. Other than she did not want him to disappear if it meant she would never see him again.

'So?' she enquired, holding down a beaming smile and aiming for pleasant.

'So I thought I'd stop by and, since you refused my invitation to lunch, see how you felt about dinner?'

Don't smile, don't smile. By a supreme effort she held the smile down. 'With you?' she asked pleasantly.

'Just me,' he confirmed. 'You've ample time to tell Dawson you can't make it.'

She had to laugh—she just did. 'Where?' she asked, her heart suddenly starting to sing.

Nathan looked pleased that she had just accepted to have dinner with him. 'Presumably you'd like to stay well away from Dawson's hotel?'

'It might be politic,' she agreed. She had, after all, turned said Dawson's dinner invitation down.

'What's wrong with here?'

Absolutely nothing! Absolutely, wonderfully nothing! 'Here would be good,' she agreed.

His eyes held hers. But a moment later he stepped back. 'I'll call for you at seven.'

That did not leave her very much time. 'Fine,' she replied, and casually stepped back into her room. Though once the door was closed she was galvanised into action. What was she going to wear? Suddenly she was starving.

She was dressed in a knee length dress of amber-gold-coloured silk when Nathan next knocked on her door. She did not keep him waiting. 'Phelix,' he said—just her name—and she went weak at the knees.

It was the start of the most wonderful evening of her life. Nathan escorted her down to the lounge area and saw she was seated on a sofa, while he took the chair to the left of her. Which suited her fine, because she was able to look at him whenever she chose. That, of course, meant that equally he could look at her, but she'd had time to give herself a small lecture that had gone along the lines of not by word, look or deed, would he know how things were with her.

An assistant came from behind the adjacent bar to enquire if they required anything. Phelix opted for a gin and tonic while Nathan had a Scotch.

'You're not in any hurry to eat?' Nathan thought to ask.

If it meant extending the hours she was with him Phelix would have been quite happy not to eat until midnight. 'Not at all,' she replied evenly. And, because she felt something else was needed, 'It's just lovely to be able to relax.'

'You still work long hours—at home?'

She smiled at him, wondered if perhaps she maybe ought to ration her smiles, but didn't seem to be able to stop herself from smiling. It was a fact: it was a joy just to be with him.

'You know how it is,' she replied, knowing for certain that a man in his position didn't just cut and run when the clock struck five.

'You enjoy your work?' Nathan asked.

'I do, actually. Mainly, I think, because I work under Henry. I've learned so much more from him since I qualified.' And, as the thought suddenly struck, 'I do work, you know. Just because I'm the boss's daughter, so to speak, I—'

'I don't doubt it,' Nathan cut in easily. 'Knowing your father I'd say you earn every penny of your salary and more.' She was feeling a little foolish. There had been no need for her to defend herself. But Nathan was giving her no time to feel a fool, and was going on, 'Whose decision was it that you should go into the firm?'

Phelix thought about it, but somehow, instinctively, she seemed to know that Nathan would not break any confidence she shared with him. 'I think it was more or less part of the deal I made with my father.' And, when Nathan looked interested to hear more, 'Well, he'd always bossed me about, as you probably know. Always been—er—a bit difficult. But as—um—difficult as he sometimes is, I just couldn't get over the way he'd gone back on his word to you.'

'Forget it,' Nathan inserted quietly, but she knew that he never would. Or forgive either, for that matter.

'Does your father know?' she asked as the impulse struck her.

'About the marriage?' Nathan studied her for a moment before replying honestly, 'I was saving that information until I could wave the cheque and tell him to stop worrying. I would have then told him how I'd earned it.' He paused. 'There didn't seem much point in upsetting him by telling him afterwards.'

'I'm sorry,' she said huskily.

'You are not the one who should apologise,' Nathan stated, his expression softening. 'Go on,' he instructed, 'what made you opt to train in law and go into the family firm?'

Phelix hesitated. 'It'll bore the socks off you.'

'I doubt you could ever do that,' Nathan said lightly, and her heart turned over.

'Well—' she started abruptly. Well—what? 'So—um—well—er—the reason I was originally so keen to have that initial ten percent of my inheritance was because to have that money would have meant I'd have the financial backing to leave home.'

Nathan did not query her being unhappy there, he must have known the answer, and stated instead, 'But you're still living there?'

Phelix began to wonder about Nathan's occasional bumping in to Henry, for the fact that she was still living at home must, she felt, have come from Henry.

'That was part of the deal. When Henry suggested I train in law and I started to get keen on the idea I knew—er...' She halted—whatever she said, her father wasn't going to come out of this sounding too good.

'You fancied training? Were keen on it?' Nathan took up. 'And?' he prompted.

She loved him. How could she hold back? 'Well, I knew I'd probably need all my inheritance to fund my training.'

Nathan, perhaps sensing she was struggling not to be disloyal to her father, for all her father had long since forfeited any right to her loyalty, made no comment on what he thought of her skinflint parent—he knew to his own cost that Edward Bradbury put money before honour.

'You paid for your own training—and stayed with your father because you couldn't afford to move out?' he enquired evenly.

'Not totally. My father went up in the air when I told him what I wanted to do.'

'He gave you a hard time?'

And then some! But she didn't want to think about that. 'The balloon went up again when I told him I was moving out.'

'He wanted you to stay home?'

'Not particularly, I don't think. But he knew that if I went Grace would leave too. She runs the house like clockwork—he'd never get another housekeeper half as good and he knew it.'

'So you stayed just so he would have a well-oiled home to live in?'

'Not totally. My conscience was plaguing me, naturally.'

'Naturally,' Nathan agreed, with a sort of gentle look for her.

Her heart acted up again, causing her to have to concentrate extra hard on what they were discussing. 'There was a lot going on at the time. Henry guiding me about training, interviews, and so on, and then there was Grace. She'd made a comfortable home for herself with us and was due to retire in a few years' time. She'd told me many times, and meant it, that when I went she was off. But was it right, with her pension not yet due, that she should start to look for other work at her age? Anyhow, when I confided in Henry he said that as I rarely saw my father I might just as well live at home as not.'

'And that was all right with you?'

'It seemed the best compromise. My father didn't like that I was determined to study law, but, as he was certain I was never going to stick it out until I qualified, he agreed.'

'He thought it would be a few months' wonder and then you'd pack it in?'

'Something like that—and I've talked quite, quite enough,'

she said firmly. Had she ever! She hadn't opened up like that to anyone—except maybe Henry—and he knew her circumstances anyway.

'You still haven't told me whose decision it was that you went into the firm,' Nathan reminded her.

She had told him everything else, she supposed she might as well add that little bit. 'My father pointed out that I would be doing the Bradbury name a great disservice if I worked anywhere else.' What he'd actually bellowed was that he wasn't having her giving some rival firm details of his business—not that she would, even had she known any. 'Anyhow, Henry wanted me with him, and I wanted to work with Henry, so we all got out of it with honour intact.' She inwardly winced—how could she mention honour and her father in the same breath in front of Nathan?

But, whatever he was thinking, Nathan refrained from saying it, and instead stated, 'You're very fond of Henry.'

'He was a great friend to my mother. He has helped me tremendously, and I love him dearly. And now I really am going to shut up,' she declared, and was determined to not say another word.

Nathan glanced at her determined expression. And smiled that smile that would have had her telling him anything he wanted to know. 'Hungry?' he asked.

They went across to the dining room and were greeted and seated and presented with a mouthwatering five-course menu. And it *was* mouthwatering, and it was the best meal, the best companion and the most magical time ever.

She discovered with her grilled tuna and vegetable salad starter that Nathan could talk on any subject. And found with the apple curry cream soup that she chose to follow that he seemed to really want to hear her opinions and ideas. They both had a green salad to follow, and never seemed to have a stilted moment.

With the beef, potato noodles and spinach they both ordered next, Nathan wanted to know what she did for pleasure, and asked lightly about her male escorts. 'I occasionally go out with someone from work. I don't seem to have a lot of time to meet anyone socially,' she replied.

'And you'd be extremely selective even then,' he stated, seeming to know that about her.

Over the final course—Phelix opted for a sorbet, about all she could manage—she asked him about his social life. 'How about you?' she asked, not certain that she wanted to know. 'Er—anyone special?'

Nathan looked at her, seemed to enjoy what he saw, and for a moment or two did not say anything, so that she began to think that perhaps she had overstepped the privacy mark. Though he hadn't hung back from asking her anything *he* wanted to know, had he?

Then suddenly he smiled and gave what seemed to her, in her in loving and not-thinking-straight mind, to be a tender look, as he answered softly, 'No one I'd want to divorce you for, Phelix.' Her heart thundered and she had to look away. How intimate he had made that sound. But in the next second, obviously having noted she had finished her sorbet, 'Coffee here or in the lounge?' he enquired.

'Lounge,' she opted. She knew she was being greedy, but if they had coffee at the table it would not take long to drink, whereas if they went into the lounge perhaps they could linger a little while longer. And the plain truth was she never wanted the evening to end.

By a mutual sort of choice they returned to the seats they had used before. The lounge was fairly deserted, she noted, and that was fine by her. Nathan ordered coffee and turned to her.

'So who was he?' he asked casually.

'Who?' She was, for the moment, completely foxed.

'Your somebody special?'

'I don't have a "somebody special",' she replied honestly.

'Shame on you,' he scolded. 'Only this morning—while we were having coffee—you told me that there nearly was someone special.'

'Honestly!' she gasped. 'Do you forget nothing?'

'Not when it was plain you were trying to avoid talking about it.'

'I'm sorry. I must have made it sound too important,' she said lightly. She didn't want to tell him about Lee Thompson, so wouldn't.

'Was it important?' Nathan persisted.

Terrier, did she say? 'If you must know, he got away.'

'This was before I came on the scene?'

She was starting to get annoyed—and did not want to be. 'Yes,' she answered shortly.

Nathan leaned forward. 'You're lovely when you're cross,' he breathed.

What could she do? She burst out laughing. And he, as if enjoying seeing her laugh, studied her for a few more moments before sitting back in his chair again.

And suddenly she could not be annoyed with him any more. 'Lee Thompson. He was the gardener's son, home from university. We were going to be married.'

Nathan's brow shot up. 'The devil you were!' he exclaimed. 'You were lovers?' he demanded.

'I thought we were, but—um—not in the actual physical sense, if that's what you mean.'

Nathan relented, taking her naïvety back then on board with a kind look, but he still wanted to know all that there was to know, and he pressed, 'What happened?'

She had already come close to falling out with Nathan and she truly did not want that. So she took a deep breath and, there being only one way to say it, said, 'My father happened.'

'He didn't want you to marry?'

'I told him that Lee and I wanted to get married—he hit the roof.'

'How soon was this before I came on the scene?' Nathan asked, and Phelix knew then that he was, with his lightning brain, well on the way to sifting it all through.

'About a couple of weeks,' she filled in.

Nathan nodded. 'Your father wouldn't want you to be permanently married to anyone,' he said. He broke off as their coffee arrived, then continued, 'He wanted you in and out of marriage fast. Which wouldn't have happened had he let you marry a man of your own choosing.'

'I worked that out later.'

'What happened to Lee?'

Phelix wrinkled her nose in distaste. 'My father paid him off—with a bonus not to contact me, so Lee said when I phoned him. My father sacked his father at the same time. It was all very unpleasant.' She took a shaky breath as she recalled it all, but ploughed determinedly on, knowing by then that Nathan wanted to hear everything. And, after the way he had been treated, she overcame her inclination to hold back. 'Anyhow, in almost the next breath my father was telling me of the ten percent I would inherit if I married before I was twenty-five.'

'And you started to smell freedom from your father's tyranny?'

She wouldn't have put it quite like that. But tyranny, she supposed, was about right. 'Well, not at first. But a couple of days later, when he said he'd found someone for me to go through a marriage ceremony with—no strings—it didn't take me long to see that with money I could leave home and make a life for myself.' She smiled wryly. 'That simple! I could kick myself now, when I think of the hard time he gave my mother, when I think of how I knew how ruthless and uncaring he could be. Yet not once did I stop to wonder what was in it for him. Or why, when he had stopped me from marrying Lee Thompson, he was promoting that I should marry someone else. I just assumed he was tired of supporting me financially.'

'You were innocent of mind and everything else,' Nathan said gently. 'Add to that you were winded by Lee Thompson's defection, not to mention you were most likely still suffering trauma over your mother's death. You wouldn't have stood a chance of not being taken to the cleaners, so to speak.'

Phelix smiled at him. She loved his gentle tone. She loved him. She caught her breath. Heavens above, she'd be drooling over him in a minute!

'Anyhow,' she said brightly, while she sought to find some kind of a brain, 'you—um—knew. You soon saw that there was more to my father promoting an annulment than was showing on the surface.'

'I didn't know the what of it,' Nathan responded. 'But when he so blatantly welshed on an agreement we had shaken hands on, I was ready to put any spoke in his wheel that I could find.'

'You decided your only recourse was to tell him he could forget about the annulment?'

Nathan nodded cheerfully. 'I was working solely on instinct,' he recalled. 'And you played along magnificently.' Oh, my word, had she ever! 'Have you told him yet?' Nathan asked.

'Told him…?'

'That an annulment was on the cards after all?' he answered, a look of humour in his eyes.

She wanted to laugh. This love, her love for him, was making her light-headed. 'I'm saving that for our next big row,' she replied solemnly. But couldn't keep it up. She just had to laugh.

Nathan stared at her for long, long moments, and then his face was splitting into the most infectious smile. 'If I asked very nicely, would you let me be the one to tell him?' he asked.

'You have a wicked streak in you, Nathan Mallory,' she informed him, and loved him like crazy—and started to get scared of what it was doing to her. 'I think I'll go now,' she stated, and could not in all truth say whether she was glad or sorry when Nathan made no move to prevent her from returning to her room.

'I'll come with you,' he agreed. 'We're on the same floor.' She glanced at his bulky keyring on the table in front of them, noting that his room was but four doors down from hers.

Together they left the lounge area and took the lift to the fifth floor. She did not want to part from him, and tried to be sensible, but sense and love, she was discovering, had little in common.

'You're staying on until next week?' she queried politely.

'Might as well,' he replied. 'You?'

'I'm flying home next Tuesday.' All at once she began to feel a little uptight and, when they'd had no trouble conversing freely all evening, suddenly found she was having to search for something to say. 'It's beautiful here, though, isn't it?'

Thankfully the lift came to a halt, and they walked the short way to her room. Nathan had to pass her door to get to his own, but as they came to a halt outside her door, and her lips started to form the words to say goodnight, Nathan asked, 'Did you love him?'

Her green eyes shot to his. 'Who?' Her head was so full of the man she had married, it seemed to have slowed down her normally quick-thinking processes.

'Thompson? You were all set to marry him, remember? Did you love him?' Nathan repeated.

'No,' she replied, valuing honesty above all else. 'I told myself I did, of course. And my pride was bruised that I could be dumped for money. But in next to no time I was very much relieved that I hadn't married him. I—didn't love him.'

'Poor sweetheart,' Nathan murmured softly, and, if that wasn't enough to melt her bones, 'I'm sorry your pride was bruised,' he added. They gazed into each other's eyes, and the next moment he bent down and kissed her.

He did not otherwise touch her. With a hand on the doorframe at either side of her he gently, lingeringly, laid his lips not on her cheek, as before, but on hers. And she—she stood transfixed, her heart thundering— And was suddenly terrified that, in the absence of him putting his arms around her, she might put her arms around him—and hold him tight.

When at last he raised his head and, looking tenderly down into her slightly bemused face, took a small step back, Phelix was ready to faint away. 'I—er—had a lot of growing up to do,' she mumbled, from some semblance of her brain.

'You have, if I may say, done that beautifully,' he commented.

And she smiled, laughed delicately in her nervousness; the sophisticated image she had been at pains to show the world was absolutely nowhere in sight. 'You say the most wonderful things,' she said lightly, and, grabbing at a 'now or never' moment, 'Goodnight, Nathan,' she added quickly.

He looked at her as if he might kiss her again—she was going to give her imagination an almighty talking to—but instead took her key from her and opened up her door. 'Goodnight, Phelix,' he answered.

She did not wait for any more, but went smartly in and closed the door. Oh—heavens! His kiss—that light, lingering, yet passionless kiss—had been mind-blowing!

In something of a daze she went further into her room. The whole wonderful evening had been mind-blowing. Dreamily she started to relive moment after moment—and then her bedside telephone rang.

Nathan! Her heartbeats picked up again. Why Nathan would be ringing her when they had only just said goodnight she hadn't a clue, but she had to take a deep and steadying breath before she picked up the instrument.

'Hello,' she said huskily—and fell to earth with one enormous crash.

'What the hell game do you think you're playing?' roared her father in a none-too-dulcet tone.

No! No! She did not want to talk to him. *He spoilt things!* She did not want to come out from this bubble of near euphoria that had encompassed her.

'Good evening to you too, Father,' she replied, with a calmness brought about by many years of practice.

'I didn't have you booked into *that* hotel!' he bellowed.

'Well, it's very nice here. Was there any special reason you wanted me to stay elsewhere?' she enquired innocently.

'I've been trying to get hold of you!' he blazed on. 'When nobody seemed to have seen you I had no recourse but to ring Ross Dawson.'

Thank you, Ross. 'What did you want to contact me for?' Well, at least her father was not pretending not to know that Ross was there.

'Do I have to have a reason?'

Most definitely! 'Is everything all right at home?'

'No, it isn't all right! Grace has given notice!'

'Grace wants to leave?' Phelix was shocked.

'She's left!' he retorted irritably.

'Grace's left? But—'

'We had a row. I told her nobody talks to me like that—and off she went!'

'You mean—you sacked her?'

'No, I don't mean that!' he snapped—and Phelix guessed that was probably right. Blow up furiously at Grace he might, but he still valued her housekeeper skills too much to want to deprive himself of them. 'What have you been doing?' he demanded. 'Ross Dawson said he'd invited you to dinner and that you'd declined!' Thank you again, Ross! 'Why?' Edward Bradbury demanded. 'Surely even *you* can see the benefits of keeping in with the Dawson clan? Surely—'

'Actually,' she cut in, starting to feel slightly nauseated that her father saw everything from a monetary angle, 'I had dinner with somebody else.' As soon as the words were out she regretted them. This was private between her and Nathan. Their evening together had been good—it had been pretty near perfect—and her father seemed to make it his business to spoil everything.

'Who with?' As she should have known, he wasn't leaving it there.

But, perhaps because of her aversion to being anything like him, with his underhand ways, or maybe after that one mighty lie eight years ago, or it was her otherwise essential honesty, but Phelix had no intention of stooping to his level.

'If you must know, I had dinner with Nathan Mallory,' she told him up front.

For all of one second there was nothing but silence. But then, with a roar that threatened to perforate her eardrum. 'Nathan Mallory's *there*!' he exploded. Vesuvius had nothing on him. 'You've dined with him *tonight*?' he exclaimed, outraged.

'Very pleasantly,' she replied, calm under fire, and far from ready to deny something she thought of as good and decent—and more than a tiny bit sensational.

'Well, you just keep away from him!' Edward Bradbury thundered.

She was twenty-six, and this man who had done absolutely nothing for her except sire her thought he could suddenly come the heavy father! 'Any particular reason why I should?' she asked—to earn more of his wrath.

'He's not to be trusted!' he had the gall to hurl at her.

Talk about the pot becalling the kettle! She was astounded. 'I think he is!' she defended, and, getting angry despite all her efforts to stay calm, 'I also think I'm old enough to make my own decisions.'

'Don't you dare…' He began to threaten, but changed rapidly to demand, 'Are you saying that should Mallory ask you out again, despite me expressly forbidding you to accept, you'd go?'

Phelix had no idea if Nathan would ask her to have dinner

with him again or not. But she had not the slightest intention of being brow-beaten by her father.

'That's exactly what I'm saying!' she retorted firmly.

And received another earful. 'We'll *bloody well* see about *that*!' Edward Bradbury shouted, and slammed down the phone.

CHAPTER FIVE

PHELIX awoke early on Thursday morning. She had not slept well, and some of the thoughts and worries that had plagued her after father's phone call were still unresolved.

She was too churned up to stay in bed, and went and took a shower, her head full of doubts, Nathan at the core. She thought of him—and knew that her father would spoil things for her with Nathan if he could. Not that there was anything to spoil, she reprimanded herself sharply. She'd had coffee with Nathan, and had enjoyed a wonderful dinner with him. He had lightly, if lingeringly, kissed her. But that could hardly be said to be any kind of a 'thing'.

She might be in love with him, but she was suddenly sure he would be amazed if he thought she had imagined anything more in that light kiss than he had intended.

And anyway, a kiss to her cheek and one light kiss to her mouth was no sort of a declaration. Nor, with her father and Lee Thompson being the two men who had attempted to mess up her life, was she anywhere certain that she wanted it to be. She might be twenty-six, but in the cold light of day she did not think she was ready for any sort of a relationship.

Self-preservation it might be, but she was wise enough to know that should the impossible happen, and Nathan might want to take things further, then she, the one in love, was the one who was going to get hurt—seriously hurt—when it came to an end.

Battling against memories of her gentle mother and the heartbreak she had suffered when she had fallen in love with Edward Bradbury, there was no way Phelix was going to go down that road. Needing to outrace her thoughts, she got into her swimsuit, donned the hotel's white bathrobe and went down to the hotel's swimming pool.

Phelix had swum ten lengths when she realised she was being ridiculous anyway. For one thing Nathan was nothing at all like her father, nor Lee Thompson. Oh, she didn't doubt that Nathan could be tough when his business demanded it, but she had seen his gentle side. But, for another, she was creating a problem where there just wasn't one. Nathan, though married to her he might be, just wasn't interested.

And that gave her pause for thought. How could he be interested when he could not possibly want to do anything that might block an easy 'out' of their marriage? *Oh!*

She had been treading water when someone swimming underwater grabbed a hold of her ankle, cutting off all thought, letting her know that she no longer had the pool to herself. But before she could sink too far under a pair of safe hands were at her waist, pulling her to the surface.

Breaking through the water, she shook her hair back from her face—to find she was looking straight into the mischievous laughing grey eyes of the man who consumed most of her thoughts.

'Good morning, Miss Bradbury,' Nathan greeted her, his hands still at her waist as they both trod water. In an instant, just seeing him negated every one of the anxieties that had awoken with her.

'You do realise it will take for ever for me to dry my hair,' she told him primly, her heart singing.

'You've nothing to hurry for,' he replied, unperturbed.

And she loved him, loved him, loved him. 'You didn't say you swam,' she commented, vaguely remembering that she had told him that she swam most mornings, but overwhelmingly aware of his broad naked chest and the dark wet hair clinging there.

'I've just taken it up,' he answered, his thighs brushing against her thighs, threatening to blow her mind.

'You brought your swimming gear with you?' And, sudden panic turning her insides over, 'You're not…?'

'In the buff?' He grinned. 'Relax, Phelix—there's a sports shop across the road.'

He'd purchased some swimming shorts yesterday! But with Nathan so near, his hard-muscled thighs brushing hers again, just the feel of his naked skin against her own skin was threatening to block out all thought.

'Well, I'd better—' she began edgily, never having imagined herself in this situation.

'Don't be alarmed, Phelix.' Nathan cut her off, every bit as if he knew that the intimacy of his near enough naked body next to hers was causing her to want to erect barriers. He let go of her. But as she swam to the side he swam to the side with her.

'I'll—er…' she began, starting to clamber out of the pool. 'I'll see you later.' That sounded too much as if she was trying to make a date with him. Oh, grief! 'At the conference—er—probably—'

'Or,' he cut in, treading water, his grey eyes taking in her long-legged shapely form prior to his gaze meeting hers, 'Or we could both bunk off and spend the day…'

Phelix abruptly turned from him. Suddenly, while happily knowing that there was nothing wrong with her shape and size, she began to feel totally vulnerable. Hastily taking up one of the towels set out for use, she wrapped it round her head and shrugged quickly into her towelling robe. Only then did she feel able to consider what was on offer.

In actual fact there was no contest. When it came to sitting in that conference hall, trying to keep her thoughts from straying, and the choice of 'bunking off' to spend the day with Nathan Mallory, the conference did not stand a chance.

Suitably towelled and robed, she took a deep breath—but went to pieces again as Nathan got out of the water too and reached for a towel. Oh, heavens, he was magnificent.

'I—er—promised I'd have lunch with Ross Dawson!' she found, out of an entirely woolly head.

'The hell you did!' Nathan rapped sharply.

'It was that or dinner last night.'

'In that case I'll forgive you,' he relented, and, with a smile that made her too weak to refuse any other offer he made, 'I've some business to take care of first. How about I call for you around ten? I'll take you to this place I know for coffee. Put your flat shoes on,' he instructed.

She thought, only briefly, of telling him of her father's call. But her father had no part in this—whatever this was. 'You're on,' she agreed, and felt a need to kiss him, and wondered if she had completely lost her senses. 'See you,' she said quickly, and got out of there.

It seemed hours to go before ten. But she put those hours to good use. She showered and shampooed her hair, used the bathroom hairdryer to good effect—but then she began to have doubts. When she was with Nathan everything seemed so right, nothing worrying or complicated. But the minute she was away from him doubts seemed to rain their spiteful darts down on her.

What she was doubting, she was not sure. Nathan wasn't asking her to rob a bank or do anything criminal. All he was asking, in the absence of her being able to spend the day with him, was that he take her for coffee—flat shoes required. Given that her father would be furious if he ever heard she wasn't 'networking', what could be more innocent than that? With any man other than Nathan she would not have wasted a moment considering the ifs, ands or buts, but would have gone along with the idea or not, as she fancied. Love, she was discovering, when at war with the strait-laced emotion-stifled austerity of her upbringing, was a string-jerking puppet master.

Deciding to leave ferreting away and not to give doubt another chance, Phelix instead channelled her thoughts to Grace. There was no way Grace could be allowed to leave just like that! Phelix determined to get in touch with her as soon as she could. Grace always made certain Phelix had her friend's telephone number whenever she went to stay with her. Midge was sure to have heard from her. Phelix decided to give Midge a ring when she was back in London.

Intent on thinking only of what she must do with regard to Grace, Phelix suddenly found she was wondering had Nathan purchased his swimwear especially because he knew that she swam most mornings? Surely not! She was being fanciful. As if he would! The poor man just felt like some exercise, that was all. For heaven's sake, get your act together!

Unsure what strange intuition was putting such weird notions into her head, Phelix left her room and went down to breakfast. She half hoped—didn't hope—that Nathan might be in the breakfast dining room. And did not know whether she was glad or sorry when there was no sign of him. Quite plainly he'd either had breakfast or was having a working breakfast in his room.

The notion that he probably felt like some exercise was borne out, though, when at ten o'clock he tapped on her door and, when she opened it, glanced down to her flat-heeled shoes and nodded approvingly.

'Fancy a walk up a mountain?' he asked.

Her lips parted in surprise. She saw him glance to her mouth—the mouth he had last night kissed—and she tried desperately to get her head together. He only had to look at her and she was just so much jelly.

'The same one we walked down yesterday?' she enquired, somehow managing to make her voice sound even. So *that* was where this place was that he knew for coffee.

'You'll enjoy it,' he stated.

It had taken them over half an hour to walk down. Heaven alone knew how much longer it would take them to walk up. 'I'm sure,' she murmured, and left the hotel with him, to walk some way along the Promenade until they found the path that would lead them ever upward.

They set off walking steadily up the zig-zag path, sometimes exchanging conversation and sometimes not. And it was all too fantastic for Phelix. She wanted to store up this time she spent with him. To enjoy it and to look back on it with no regrets. She would be leaving on Tuesday—it was highly unlikely that she would see him again after that.

She had been reluctant to attend the conference, but these last two days—yesterday and today—had been magical. Yesterday Nathan had followed her…

'Yesterday,' she plunged, before she had thought it through—and was then committed to going on. 'Given that I've talked and talked about my side of our—er—marriage bargain…' She wished she hadn't got started, but too late now—she would look foolish if she stopped. 'Was that why you followed me? Because you wanted to know about why I work for my father—about…er…?' Her voice tailed off. Of course it was, idiot! What else could it have been? Heavens, she had talked so much he must have had earache.

'Tell me about Henry,' Nathan suggested, before she should feel more idiotic than she already did.

That stopped her dead in her tracks. 'Henry Scott?' she stood rooted to ask.

Nathan halted too. 'Henry Scott,' he agreed.

'Henry…' She began to walk on, and Nathan fell into step with her. At first she thought he had thrown Henry into the conversation because, perhaps noticing that she was feeling a little foolish, he was merely changing the subject.

But, glancing at Nathan, she saw there was something in the

serious look of him that seemed to more than suggest to her that his question about Henry was not without purpose, that he really wanted to know about him.

'Was Henry some of the reason you followed me yesterday?' she asked. With Nathan looking so sort of determined somehow, it struck her then that Henry seemed to have a great deal to do with why Nathan had followed her. Though for the life of her she couldn't think why.

'I'd like to hear more about him.'

'You do know that Henry has my absolute loyalty…?'

'As I suspect you have his,' Nathan inserted.

'True,' she agreed, and, that established, 'So what do you want to know that, given those parameters, I can tell you?'

'You said you loved him, and I've taken it as a two-way feeling.'

That seemed to her to be more about her and Henry than just Henry. But she could see no reason not to reply. 'Henry looked out for my mother. He…'

'They were having an affair?'

'No!' Phelix exclaimed sharply. But calmed down to add, 'No, I'm sure not. It was just that, well, her life wasn't easy. She was much too gentle a person to be married to a man like my father. And Henry—he was always sort of there for her. He recognised that gentleness in her, and cared for her. When she died he transferred that caring on to me.' Phelix broke off as she recalled the many times that Henry had metaphorically held her hand. 'I'd have been lost without Henry so many times. Not just in business, but things were pretty bleak when my mother died. He always seemed to be there in my down moments.'

'Not your father?'

As if! 'What's your interest in Henry?' she asked, ignoring the question. Nathan knew the answer anyway, she felt sure.

'He knows,' Nathan replied.

'Who knows?'

'Henry.'

'Knows what?' she queried, having lost him somewhere.

'Henry Scott knows that I'm the man you married,' he stated, as if he absolutely knew that for a fact.

That stopped her dead in her tracks again. 'He can't know!' she protested. 'I didn't tell him—didn't tell anybody!' Nathan still looked absolutely certain. 'How do you think you know he knows?' she challenged, winded by just the thought of it.

They had come to a halt by a thoughtfully placed bench. Nathan took hold of her arm and led her over to it. By unspoken mutual consent they took their ease on it. 'Something you said on Tuesday set me thinking,' he said, to enlighten her.

From where Phelix was seeing it, she hadn't a clue what she had said on Tuesday that had given him pause to think that Henry knew the name of the man she had married. 'When we were in that park next to the conference centre?' she asked, realising that it had to be there, because apart from exchanging a few courtesy words of greeting on Tuesday morning they hadn't had any other conversation that day. Nathan nodded confirmation anyway, and she just had to ask, 'What? What did I say that set you thinking?'

Nathan looked into the distance. It was another beautiful day, the view as magnificent as ever. 'A couple of things, actually,' he responded after a few seconds. 'You said Henry knew you were very upset over the way your marriage partner had been treated. You also said that Henry seemed to know everyone and…'

'You thought from that that Henry had guessed the name of the man I'd married the day before?' How, for goodness' sake?

'Not then—that was a side issue,' Nathan replied. 'But when I tied it in with other matters—that he should know my name and want to do something on your behalf to honour a deal that you, by the sound of it, were feeling so wretched about—it all started to slot in most convincingly.'

'It's been said,' Phelix chipped in dryly, 'that I have quite a bright head on my shoulders. So why haven't I a clue what you're talking about?'

Nathan turned and gave her that half smile that turned her bones to water. 'Probably because you don't know the half of it,' he said softly.

Oh, Nathan! Swiftly she stiffened her limpid spine. 'But you're going to tell me?'

He nodded. 'I've been examining the facts. One—Henry thinks the world of you. Two—he knew you were upset. I'm sure you would have confided in him about the Lee Thompson affair?' Phelix nodded confirmation, and Nathan went on. 'From that Henry would know that your father had sold you twice—or would have, had he not shot himself in the foot, so to speak, by not paying up the second time. Point three—and I'm guessing here—you told Henry how you'd offered me all of that ten percent of your inheritance and—'

'I did—and that you'd refused to take it.'

Nathan took that on board, and said, 'From my small dealings with Henry Scott, I would say that he is a most honourable man.'

'He is!' Phelix exclaimed. 'He's one of the finest men I know.'

Nathan gave a brief nod. 'Which would make him want to do whatever he could on your behalf to repair the situation.'

'You think so?'

'I've been certain of it ever since Tuesday,' Nathan replied.

'When I said Henry knew I was upset over the way you were treated?'

'And how Henry seemed to know everyone,' Nathan confirmed, going on, 'You may remember that your father and the deal I made with him was my last-ditch desperate attempt to save my company…'

'Oh, Nathan!'

'Don't!' he said sharply. 'You are in no way to blame.' She wanted to say thank you, but suddenly felt too choked to speak. 'Anyhow, I was sunk, or thought I was. My father and I were on the verge of ruin with nothing more I could do about it. Then, just two days later with just about twenty-four hours to go before I must make an announcement that Mallory and Mallory were finished, a note was delivered to my home that started to give me hope.'

'A note?' she repeated, starting to be even more intrigued. 'Who from?'

'It was unsigned. I never discovered who from,' he answered. 'By the time I'd read it, the despatch rider who had delivered it was roaring away on his motorbike.' He paused for a moment to mention, 'In those early days I was too busy getting the firm afloat again to over-worry about who had sent it.'

'You just got on with it, head down, no time to look at side issues?'

'That's about it,' Nathan acknowledged. 'I've wanted many times in more recent years to find out who sent that note, but the trail has long gone cold,' he revealed. And then he asked, 'Ever heard of a man named Oscar Livingstone?'

Who hadn't? 'He's some sort of arts philanthropist—er—a theatre backer,' she replied. And added innocently, quite unprepared for Nathan's reaction, 'Henry was up at Oxford with him.'

'I *knew* it!' Nathan exclaimed, and suddenly she was feeling the benefit of his full smile head on. 'I *knew* it!' he repeated, and the next she knew Nathan had caught a hold of her shoulders, pulled her to him, and was planting an exuberant kiss on her slightly parted lips.

She had to smile, she just had to. 'I wish I *knew* it,' she said lightly, feeling quite bemused.

And could not believe it when Nathan divulged, 'Oscar Livingstone at that time—totally unbeknown to me or to anyone who didn't know him well—was also looking to invest in a company that, while having potential to go places, was struggling to make it.'

She stared at him wide-eyed. 'Oscar Livingstone invested in your company?' she asked, startled.

'We could never have made it without him.'

'But…' She was stunned.

'Exactly! How did he hear about us? My father and I had been keeping the state of our finances very quiet. Only obviously your father somehow knew how truly dire our situation was.'

'And my father was unlikely to put your name—his competitor—forward.'

'Understatement of the year,' Nathan commented shortly, but added, 'Oscar Livingstone would not reveal who it was who had put our name forward. But it was your man Henry. I'm convinced of it.'

Phelix would love it to have been Henry, but did not see how it could have been. 'H-how…?' She was too shaken to work it out, but tried anyway. 'I mentioned on Tuesday that Henry seemed to know everyone.' She went through it piece by piece. 'I also said how I'd told Henry how very upset I was over the way you had been treated. And…'

'And Henry, I'm guessing, would want to do whatever he could to put that right for you.' Nathan helped her out.

'You think so?'

'I'm sure of it the more I think about it. And for all I was initially too over-worked to have time to do anything but be grateful that somebody else *had* interfered, I've never forgotten or ceased to be grateful.'

'But—how…?'

'How did he know it was me you had married the day before?' Nathan asked, and answered, 'By the simplest of methods. He had the date; all he had to do was nip into the register office and ask to see the current register to find out who. In no time he would have discovered not only the name of the man who had been married to Phelix Elizabeth Bradbury on that date, but also the man's home address and his occupation—the rest of his enquiries would follow on easily.'

'Good heav… Why didn't I think of that?'

'There was no need for you to think of it. As it was, without your knowing it, by confiding everything to Henry you did more than repair the damage. A day afterwards, presumably after Henry had checked me out, I received an anonymous note saying, "Oscar Livingstone is waiting to take your call." There followed what I now know to be Oscar Livingstone's private telephone number.'

'You rang it?'

'I was desperate. If it was a hoax, so be it. I rang it,' Nathan confirmed, 'and was never more glad that I did when the great man invited my father and I in for a chat.'

'He backed you?'

'He backed us, but refused to be drawn as to who had told him about us.'

Phelix looked at him with shining eyes. 'It had to be Henry,' she said.

'That's what I think,' Nathan answered with a gentle look for her. He stretched out a hand as though about to touch her face. But abruptly drew back and got to his feet. 'Coffee,' he said decisively.

Together they climbed the rest of the way up to the restaurant area. Each busy with their own thoughts, they said little.

Phelix's head was full of what Nathan had told her. Henry—good, kind, wonderful Henry. He had known how very dreadful she had been feeling about Nathan, had known when she had told him how she had offered Nathan all of her ten percent that she would want to do anything she could to recompense him. And by the simplest of methods, having discovered the name of the man she had married—for she had only said that the man she'd married was a businessman undergoing severe financial problems—Henry had done what he could to fully redeem her honour.

They reached the plateau and, the sun shining brilliantly, again opted to have their coffee outside. 'I'm still trying to take it in,' she said as the waitress brought their coffee.

'You'll adjust,' Nathan assured her.

'Have you?' she asked. 'You've had two days in which to get your head together. Have you adjusted yet?'

'More settled than adjusted, I think,' Nathan replied. And then asked, 'Is this just between you and me, Phelix?'

She thought about it. It was such a wonderful thing Henry had done, she did not think she could just—let it go. 'May I not thank Henry?' she questioned sincerely.

'You'd keep it to yourself just for me?' Nathan asked, his grey eyes warm on her green ones.

'If you insist,' she replied quietly, her heart starting to pound at the warmth in his look for her.

Nathan did not insist, but asked, 'Would you let me know when you've thanked him?' And her heart pounded the more. Because she had been certain that after next Tuesday, if not before, all her contact with Nathan would end. But here he was, asking that she let him know, and since she would not have chance to personally thank Henry until she went into the office the following Wednesday, she would at least be in telephone contact with Nathan. 'I'd like to thank him myself.'

'Of course,' she murmured.

Her defences were already down, she was ready to melt under Nathan's warm regard, and so was rendered utterly speechless when, quite out of the blue, 'Would you take my heart, Phelix?' he asked softly.

With her own heart thundering against her ribs, she stared at him. But, confusion reigning, she had to glance away. Down to the table—which in actual fact was most fortunate. Because only then was she able to see the plastic-wrapped heart-shaped biscuit he was offering.

Not trusting her voice, she shook her head. Oh, what an idiot love had made her! As if Nathan would ever truly offer her his heart! It took her a few moments to gather sufficient control to be able to murmur lightly, 'Don't want to spoil my appetite for lunch.' She flicked a glance to his face and saw that his warm look had disappeared, to be replaced by a stern look. She thought for one inane moment that he was annoyed, or jealous, even, that she was lunching with Ross Dawson.

Her imagination was having one hysterically mad field-day, she soon realised. Honestly! Though she felt a little better when, his stern look gone, 'I refuse to allow you to have lunch *and* dinner with Dawson,' Nathan told her forthrightly.

Was he asking her to have dinner with him that night? Oh what should she do? What she did—since the only communication she might have with Nathan after she left Switzerland would be that telephone call to confirm that she had thanked Henry—was to decide at that very moment that she was going to see as much as she possibly could of Nathan, and enjoy every second of it.

'If you're very good, I'll take you to dinner tonight,' she invited prettily.

He stared into her laughing eyes. 'Call for me at seven,' he accepted.

Shortly afterwards Phelix glanced at her watch. 'I'd better start making tracks,' she said lightly. She knew she was being greedy, but she did not want to start 'making tracks.' She wanted to spend more time with Nathan. She looked at him, this man she had married, and her insides somersaulted. 'I'd—er—better take the funicular down,' she added brightly, striving for some sort of normality, striving to hide the least suspicion of a love-light in her eyes.

Together they descended, and well within the next ten minutes they were standing together on the pavement of the Promenade. 'Coming this way?' Nathan asked when she hesitated. He was half turned towards the conference centre.

She denied herself the pleasure. 'I'd better pop back to the hotel and freshen up.'

Nathan looked at her long and hard. 'You do realise that

you're my wife,' he murmured, more as though to himself than to her—and her heart started playing a merry tune once more.

'Which leaves me with certain privileges,' she answered lightly. And some creature within her with whom she had never been acquainted before suddenly took charge, and Phelix did no more than reach up and kiss him—and did not know which one of them was the more surprised, him or her. 'Er—thanks for the coffee,' she said quickly, and turned hastily about.

She was still wondering about this new and impulsive creature love had turned her into when she reached the sanctuary of her room. Good heavens, they just weren't 'kissing' husband and wife! Though it was true Nathan had kissed her a couple of times.

But she must not read anything into that, she counselled, as she changed into a smart trouser suit and a crisp white shirt. Not that she wanted 'anything' to *be* in it.

As before, Phelix stated to worry about her friendship with Nathan. Everything seemed so right when she was with him. But the moment they parted she began to wonder if she had given away her feelings for him. She would just die if she had, and did not doubt that if Nathan had seen how she felt about him, he would be consulting a divorce lawyer the first chance he had.

He did not want her love. And, on thinking about it, she did not want to give it to him. She knew that she didn't have too much faith in men—though she would never forget Nathan's gentleness with her on their wedding night, or rather, the night following their marriage. She found she was wondering what kind of a lover he would be—and hastily brought herself up short.

Good heavens! What on earth was going on in her head? All his fault of course, but he did have the most wonderful mouth! She recalled his bare chest down at the pool that morning, his long straight legs when he'd got out of the pool and stood with her, water hanging on one of his nipples. For heaven's sake…!

The Harlequin Reader Service — Here's how it works:

Accepting your 2 free books and 2 free gifts (gifts valued at approximately $10.00) places you under no obligation to buy anything. You may keep the books and gifts and return the shipping statement marked "cancel." If you do not cancel, about a month later we'll send you 6 additional books and bill you just $3.32 each for the regular-print edition or $3.82 each for the larger-print edition in the U.S. or $3.80 each for the regular-print edition or $4.30 each for the larger-print edition in Canada. That is a savings of at least 15% off the cover price. It's quite a bargain! Shipping and handling is just 25¢ per book. You may cancel at any time, but if you choose to continue, every month we'll send you 6 more books, which you may either purchase at the discount price or return to us and cancel your subscription.

*Terms and prices subject to change without notice. Prices do not include applicable taxes. Sales tax applicable in N.Y. Canadian residents will be charged applicable provincial taxes and GST. Offer not valid in Quebec. Credit or debit balances in a customer's account(s) may be offset by any other outstanding balance owed by or to the customer. Please allow 4 to 6 weeks for delivery. Offer available while quantities last.

If offer card is missing write to: Harlequin Reader Service, 3010 Walden Ave., P.O. Box 1867, Buffalo NY 14240-1867

NO POSTAGE NECESSARY IF MAILED IN THE UNITED STATES

BUSINESS REPLY MAIL
FIRST-CLASS MAIL PERMIT NO. 717 BUFFALO, NY

POSTAGE WILL BE PAID BY ADDRESSEE

HARLEQUIN READER SERVICE
3010 WALDEN AVE
PO BOX 1867
BUFFALO NY 14240-9952

As if to escape the demons that had been nowhere a part of her until she had become reacquainted with Nathan Mallory, Phelix hastily left her room.

She went quickly along the Promenade and decided that she would cancel her dinner date with Nathan that night. Then she countermanded that notion. Botheration, she loved him! Tuesday would come too soon, and with it her return to England. She should be glad about that. Perhaps once she was back in her old routine everything would settle down again.

But she had tasted the uplift of spirits that came each time she saw the man she loved. The welter of emotions, highs and lows, that came with being with him and with not being with him. Life, she knew, was going to be very dull when she lost all chance of seeing Nathan again.

She half wished that she had not come to Davos. That she had not seen him again. Were it not for one of his scientists being unable to make the trip, she would not have seen him.

But how could she half-wish anything of the kind? Until she had fallen in love with him she had been asleep. Falling in love with Nathan had brought her awake—made her feel alive. Just thinking about him made her…

But she would settle down again. She would have to, she resolved. She had a good career. Under Henry's guidance… Oh, how could she ever have forgotten Henry? Dear, kind, good Henry. It was the things Henry did, the way he behaved, that time and time again had restored her faith that there were good men around.

Instinctively she wanted to telephone him and thank him from the bottom of her heart for what he had done. She somehow knew without question that it was Henry who had instigated the saving of Mallory and Mallory.

But this was too big for a telephone call. She needed to thank him in person. And would, the first chance she had.

Meantime, she had to meet Ross Dawson for lunch. Only

somehow lunch with Ross did not have the same thrill as dinner with Nathan. 'Call for me at seven,' he had said.

A smile curved her lips—she could hardly wait.

CHAPTER SIX

HER lunch with Ross Dawson was a pleasant enough affair. 'I didn't see you at the conference this morning?' he more enquired than commented as soon as they were seated.

'Was it interesting?' Phelix evaded. There was no reason why she could not have told him that she had walked a good way up a mountain to have a cup of coffee. But he might ask who with, and somehow her time with Nathan was special and private.

'It'll be more interesting next week when the top boys from JEPC Holdings hit town.'

'So I believe,' she replied. If Ross was fishing to find out how much she knew then he was going to be disappointed. Apart from the fact that she knew only the bare bones of the outsourcing contract that was said to be in the offing, she did, regardless of her father's doubts, have a certain loyalty to her father's company.

'Did your father manage to get you last night?' Ross, seeing he was getting nowhere with his feelers, changed the subject.

'He did. Thanks for letting him know where to find me,' she answered lightly. There was no need for Ross to know that her relationship with her father was not what she would have wished. She had not forgotten her father's furious 'We'll see about that!' when she'd said she would go out with Nathan Mallory again should he ask her. Though what he thought he could do about it, she failed to see.

She and Ross chatted amicably through their meal. But as they left the dining room, 'Fancy dodging out of the conference this afternoon?' he asked.

'What sort of a girl do you think I am?' she asked, and had to laugh when Ross replied he knew what sort of a girl he'd like her to be.

Her laughter died when, out of nowhere, it seemed, there was Nathan Mallory! She saw him favour Ross Dawson with a stern look, though he was quite pleasant to him when he asked, 'Good lunch?'

'Depends who you're with,' Ross replied with a warm look to her.

Nathan gave a small inclination of his head to acknowledge her, and walked on by. Somehow, her insides in knots again just from seeing him, Phelix carried on walking as if she hadn't a care in the world. But she was giving serious thought to going home to England. It had been less than a couple of hours since she had last seen him, for goodness' sake, and just seeing him again was making her feel all over the place. She had grown used to being the one in control of her life, but that control appeared to be slipping. It was very off-putting!

She saw Nathan again that afternoon. He was with other people but glanced over to her, and seemed about to smile. Phelix inclined her head a little to return the compliment, and saw him grin—and felt a huge mirthful grin of her own coming on; her lips tweaked but she hastily looked away. Honestly—what was this man doing to her?

Having deflected Ross Dawson's hope that she would have dinner with him that night, Phelix left the conference at the end of the afternoon session and—deny it though she might try, toy with the notion of haring back to England though she had—she knew that she wanted nothing more than to see Nathan again. And, joy of joys, in a very few hours that was exactly what she would do.

She walked smartly back to her hotel, wishing she had brought a more extensive wardrobe with her. Perhaps tomorrow she would cut the conference—her father would have a fit—and go in search of a dress shop.

She was taking a shower when she started to laugh at herself for her own idiocy. Oh, my word. Nathan hadn't even asked her out tomorrow evening, and already she was planning to update her wardrobe! Serve her right if he decided that dinner two nights in succession was more than enough. And yet that grin this afternoon, and her response to it. Was it just she who had felt a moment of magic in the air between them?

Her phone was ringing as she left the bathroom. She paused, took time out to swallow down a spasm of nervousness—it might just be him—and picked up the phone.

'Hello?' she enquired nicely—and had her dream shattered!

'Phelix?' Edward Bradbury barked.

Her father! Her spirits plummeted. 'Yes,' she replied.

'You'd better come along here and meet me,' he ordered.

She sank down on the bed, his 'We'll see about that' of last night taking on ominous reality. 'Where—are you?' she managed to ask, hoping against hope.

'In the hotel where you're supposed to be!'

'You've flown in…?'

'We've important business to discuss. You can have your dinner here. We'll—'

She started to recover. 'I've already arranged to have dinner elsewhere.'

'Perhaps you didn't hear me. We have business to discuss!'

'Perhaps you didn't hear *me*. I'm having dinner here.'

There was a moment's tense silence. 'Very well,' Edward Bradbury agreed disagreeably, and she thought for one lovely moment that he was giving in. She should have known better. Because, shrewdly taking it that she was not intending to dine alone, 'You'd better get your hotel to change your reservation to dinner for three,' he rapped.

Sadly, she had never been able to grow to like him, and just then she positively disliked him. 'I'll come to you,' she said woodenly, and could have wept.

Having yet again established his power to manipulate, he had nothing more to say, and Phelix put down her phone knowing that to give in had been the only thing she could have done. To share dinner with Nathan *and* her father was unthinkable. And, after the way her father had behaved to Nathan, she was astounded that he would have had the gall to impose himself on their table—for there was no doubt in her mind that her father knew that she had planned to dine again with the man he had arranged for her to marry.

She took off her robe and dressed without enthusiasm in the green dress she had worn two nights ago, when she had dined with Ross Dawson.

Hastily pulling a brush through her hair, she knew she should not delay in contacting Nathan to tell him of her change of plan. She had no idea of how he would react—more than likely shrug his shoulders and arrange to dine with someone else. But what option did she have? Her father would spoil everything. And, while she had little idea of what 'everything' was, all she knew was that she wanted to laugh with Nathan again and be happy just to be with him again—and that just wasn't going to happen with her father present.

She thought about telephoning Nathan, but, perhaps because she was already hungry for the sight of him again, she opted to go along to his room.

His room was but a few steps down from her own, but she had started to feel anxious before she had taken more than a couple of paces in that direction.

She knocked on his door and endeavoured to put a 'not too much put out' expression on her face. Nathan, shirt and trouser-clad, came to the door. She thought he was about to smile when he saw her, but he did not, so she concluded he had either not been going to smile or had picked up that something was a trifle amiss.

'Would you like to come in while I get my shoes on?' he enquired, when for the moment she had lost her voice.

He thought she had come early to call for him! 'I—er—can't make dinner after all!' she found her voice to tell him in a rush. Oh, how dear he was to her; she could have cried.

Still he did not smile but studied her face for a second or so before enquiring, 'Had a better offer?'

She supposed that was preferable than his just saying fine and closing the door in her face.

'M-my father's here,' she stammered, wanting it said and done—though she did not care at all for the hostile expression with which Nathan greeted the news.

He said nothing, however, of the fact that Edward Bradbury was in town about five days early, but queried, 'Here? At this hotel?'

'No, no,' Phelix replied.

But before she could go on, 'And this has got what, exactly, to do with me?' Nathan asked coolly—and something inside her froze.

She had said what she had come to say. There was nothing more she could add. Pride came to her aid and up went her chin. 'Not a thing,' she replied, her tone coldly aloof, and turned abruptly about and went quickly back to her own room. His door had slammed hard shut before she got there.

It was the end, and she knew it. She was dining with her father because she did not want him to spoil this—this nebulous thing, this, her time with Nathan. But it was spoilt already. Nathan was unlikely to ask her to dine with him again. And, after the way he had just so decisively closed the door, neither would she ask him.

She drove to her father's hotel, wanting her dinner with him to be over and done with as quickly as possible. She could barely remember the last time she and her father had sat down and shared a meal together—and they lived in the same house!

He was in the lounge studying some papers when she went in. There were other people there who must know who he was, but—and she thought it was so sad—her father was sitting alone.

Although, on reflection, anyone who approached him when he was reading through matters financial was bound to receive short shrift.

'Father,' she said, standing in front of him.

He did not stand up to kiss her cheek in greeting—she'd have died on the spot if he had. But, indicating the seat opposite, 'Sit down,' he said.

'Good journey?' she enquired politely. She should have known better. They just did not do small talk.

'What's Mallory doing here?' he demanded, and was at his churlish worst.

'The same as you, I shouldn't wonder,' she responded—other fathers doted on their daughters; fat chance!

'I forbid you to see him again,' he attempted brusquely.

'You gave up the right to forbid me to do anything on the day I married him and ceased to be your responsibility!' she answered, her tone low. She was conscious, unlike him, of other people around.

'Hmmph,' he grunted, and still trying to bully her, 'While you're living under my roof—' he began, but stopped when—as a new and wonderful thought suddenly struck her—Phelix's expression lightened and she started to smile.

'If I can't persuade Grace to come back, it could be I won't be living under your roof for very much longer,' she stated.

'Don't be ridiculous!'

She refused to be crushed. 'Look, do we need to carry on with this farce of a dinner?'

'You've cancelled your arrangement with Mallory?' She nodded—and saw from what passed as his smile that she had at last done something to please her father. The smile did not last. 'So what have you discovered?' he wanted to know.

'About what?'

'You've been here since Monday! Surely you've picked up something about what's going off with the outsourcing deal?'

Now did not seem an appropriate time to tell him that not only had she cut quite a few of the speeches and lectures, but also had not mingled to eavesdrop. 'Everyone seems to be playing their cards very close to their chests,' she replied instead. And, thinking of the evening she had given up and the limited chances she would have of seeing Nathan now that her father was here, she was suddenly totally fed up with this verbal sparring. 'You said you had business you wanted to discuss. What business would that be?' she enquired, knowing in advance that her father was far more likely to arrange a meeting with Henry than with her on anything to do with matters legal.

Her father looked away from her, someone just coming in catching his eye. 'Ah, here's Ross!' he exclaimed, a welcoming smile on his face. 'I've invited him to join us.'

It would not have taken much for Phelix to walk out there and then. She had given up her evening with Nathan in order to avoid an unpleasant threesome dinner at her hotel, and all along her father had planned this! If nothing else, it was embarrassing.

Good manners instilled in her by her mother came to her aid. 'Surprised to see me?' Ross asked, his eyes twinkling with pleasure at her father's invitation that he join them.

'Always a joy to see you, Ross,' she replied, and did not know if she was glad or sorry that he was there. With Ross in attendance there was no way her father was going to discuss business. On the other hand, since she and her father had never gone in for small talk, Ross's presence might help the evening along.

But oh, how much better the evening would have been had

she not had to come here at all! Had she followed her instinct she would have got out of there there and then, leaving her father with Ross for a dinner companion—that would obviate her father turning up at her hotel. But, the die cast, she could hardly speed back to her hotel and knock on Nathan's door and tell him that their dinner together was on after all. Besides, after his cool 'And this has got what, exactly, to do with me?' there was no way her pride would allow her to do anything of the sort. And in any case, he would by now most likely have found himself another dinner companion.

Phelix did not like that last thought, and so turned to Ross and tried to pretend that she was glad they had met up again.

She discovered that she had little appetite for food, but while her father and Ross skated around business issues she entered the conversation whenever she felt called upon to do so. But her heart wasn't in it. Her mind for the most part was back at the Schweizerhof with Nathan. The whole of her heart back there with him.

They were midway through their main course when such a terrible yearning came over her to be with Nathan that when she saw him enter the dining room she thought for a moment that it was purely her imagination that had conjured him up.

But it was not her imagination, it was him and, after a dark glance to her table when he surveyed her two escorts, he did no more than start to make his way over to them.

Her heart rejoiced. Her insides might be acting up like nobody's business, but her heart rejoiced just to see him. He was on his own, not a blonde, a redhead or a brunette of her imaginings in sight. Would he ignore her? Should she ignore him? Would he walk by without a word?

She averted her gaze, adopted a distant air as if it mattered not one single bit to her if he ignored her. But, while she was very much aware of him nearing their table, she would not have been at all surprised had he arrogantly walked on by.

But he did not walk past, and nor did he ignore her. And, 'hile her insides were having one wild time within her, he did o more than stop directly at their table.

Ignoring her father, he nodded briefly to Ross, and then, his ark expression disappearing as he transferred his gaze to her, Meet me for a drink after your dinner,' he invited.

Her heart was pounding so loudly she was surprised no one ould hear it. As it was, she had about one second in which to rgive him his previous cool manner with her before he strode n. She loved him—love forgave all.

'That would be—nice,' she accepted. Nice! It would be narvellous!

But as usual her father was there, to attempt to exert his ower over her. 'My daughter has business to discuss. It will e too late…'

Nathan ignored him and, to make her insides flip, he caught hold of her left hand. And did no more than lift it to his lips nd, exactly where her wedding band rested, he kissed it. 'I'll 'ait,' he said, and was gone.

Phelix was still on cloud nine, and her father still furious, o it was Ross who was the first to recover from the small ut unexpected scene. 'How well do you know Nathan Iallory?' he asked, looking a shade put out that she had greed to have a drink with another man while she was ining with him.

'As Nathan mentioned, we know each other from way back.'

'You two have history?' Ross wanted to know.

'Good heavens, no!' Edward Bradbury chipped in. 'Phelix just too polite to say no to one of our competitors.'

'She's said no to me,' Ross grumbled.

'She's just playing hard to get,' Edward Bradbury mollified im, as though she wasn't there. Phelix cared not—Nathan had orgiven her, he was no longer cool towards her, and, best yet, he would see him later.

Though, if her father had anything to do with it, later would be too late. He was in no hurry to finish his meal, and was insistent that they had an after-dinner brandy or two.

'I'm driving,' she refused.

'Then you'll stay and have coffee,' he asserted. And for Ross's benefit, 'Your poor old dad hasn't seen you all week!'

Feeling sickened at the hypocrisy of it, only good manners in front of Ross Dawson prevented her from telling her 'poor old dad' that she didn't remember seeing much of him the previous week, or the week before that for that matter.

But, given that she was yearning to be elsewhere, Ross Dawson was good company, and as they returned to the lounge he gave Edward Bradbury colourful highlights of some of the speakers and their speeches.

'You must be tired after your journey.' Phelix addressed her father when she thought, all proprieties observed, that she had spent a long enough time with them. If she didn't get a move on Nathan would begin to think she had changed her mind about having that drink with him. She had assumed, in fact was pretty certain, that he had meant that drink to be back at their hotel. She just could not bear to think that he might have given up on her and gone to bed.

'Not at all!' her father answered robustly.

'Well, I'd better make tracks…'

'I've brought some paperwork with me I need to go through with you,' he announced. Phelix looked pointedly at her watch.

It had gone eleven-thirty by the time she thought she had been quite polite enough. She had said goodnight to Ross and had accompanied her father to his suite, where he had shown her paperwork she had already seen and then discussed at great length pieces of work that were entirely nothing to do with her. All, she knew, in an attempt to prevent her from having that drink with Nathan Mallory.

Frustrated by the nonsense of it beyond bearing, she told her father bluntly that she saw little point in delaying going back to her hotel.

'What about Ross Dawson?' he demanded.

'What about him?'

'He wants to marry you! It would be a tremendous advantage to—'

'Forget it, Father. I will never, *ever* marry Ross Dawson.'

'You're being unreasonable!' Edward Bradbury erupted angrily. 'Ross is a fine man. He'll—'

'I'm well aware of what Ross is,' she butted in. 'And I agree that he's a fine man. But he's not my man. I will *not*,' she emphasised, 'ever marry him.'

'You'd rather stay married to that—that—'

Her father was starting to grow apoplectic. 'His name is Nathan Mallory,' she interrupted him calmly. 'And I'm going—'

'You're going back to have a drink with him!' he blasted her, outraged at not getting his own way, furious at the fading picture of Bradbury, Dawson and Cross.

'If he hasn't got tired of waiting.'

'Let's hope he has,' he spat. 'He's no good to you!'

And you are? 'Goodnight, Father,'

'Watch him—he'll stop at nothing get back at me!' he rapped, and, when that did not dent her, 'You be here first thing in the morning!' he ordered, and turned his back on her.

It was nearing midnight when Phelix, her car parked, entered her hotel. She felt near to tears knowing that she would be wasting her time going to the bar. Nathan would not be there.

He wasn't in the bar. Where he was, was in the adjoining lounge area. Hardly believing it, she saw him stand up as soon as he saw her, and she hurried over to him, her heart singing.

'I didn't think you'd be here!' she said in a rush.

'I said I'd wait,' he replied, his eyes taking in the anxiety in her eyes. 'Come and sit down,' he suggested, and a second or two later they were seated where they had been the previous evening. 'What would you like to drink?'

In point of fact she did not want a drink. But neither did she want to cut short her chance to spend some time with him. 'Perhaps a coffee,' she answered.

They both had coffee, Nathan seeming to be as pleased that she was there as she was to be there. 'You knew your father was on his way here?' he asked, civilly enough, but she sensed a hint of censure behind his question.

She did not want to be bad friends with him ever. She shook her head. 'He rang last night, when I got to my room. Er—Grace, our housekeeper, has finally had enough and has walked out.'

Nathan took that in, and asked, 'He told you he would arrive today?'

Again she shook her head and, realising Nathan could be thinking she'd had all the time in the world to mention it that morning, 'No,' she replied.

'So—he arrived completely out of the blue?'

'Do all your coffee companions get this third degree?' Her father had given her one grilling. Love Nathan though she might, she did not fancy another.

Nathan looked at her steadily for several long seconds then, quite clearly, stated quietly, 'Only the ones I care about.'

Oh, Nathan—her heart kicked off a riot. 'Oh, that's all right, then,' she murmured as nonchalantly as she was able. Oh, my word! Though don't read too much into that, she instructed. He wasn't intimating that she was anyone special, just one of his—many, she was sure—female coffee-drinking companions.

'Did you happen to mention, during your conversation with him last night, that I was in the vicinity?' Nathan wanted to know.

She had to give him top marks. Though guessed he was far from blinkered where her father was concerned. 'I might have mentioned that I'd had dinner with you,' she replied lightly.

'I bet he loved that,' he commented, and asked, 'Are you having dinner with him and Dawson again tomorrow?'

'Not if I can help it!' she replied promptly, but confessed, 'Actually, it was either I joined my father at his hotel or he would have come to dinner here.' And, hurrying on, 'I didn't know Ross would be there tonight.'

'Your father wants you to marry Dawson?'

'That's hardly likely with a Mallory blocking the way,' she commented, knowing that Nathan would appreciate the subtleties that while she was married to him her father's plans didn't even get off the starting blocks.

'Always a pleasure to be of use,' he remarked, his lips twitching. But, sobering, 'You're not interested in Dawson—that way?'

'I like him; he's good company. But, no, I'll never marry him,' she replied, and learned something else about the man she was married to—he seemed to have an unerring instinct about that which he did not know. Although she supposed she already knew that from eight years ago when, without knowing why, he had known that annulment was important to her father for some reason. 'He's asked you, though? Dawson? He's keen to marry you?' And, when she did not answer, 'He's in love with you?'

'I—er—don't think I feel too comfortable discussing how someone else feels about me,' she replied. 'It—er—doesn't seem fair.'

Nathan looked at her solemnly for a moment or two, and then smiled that smile that melted her bones. 'Do you know something, Phelix Bradbury, you are one rather special person.'

She looked away from him, her insides dancing a jig. He cared a little for her—he'd more or less said so. And now this, that she was one rather special person. It was all too much.

'Well—um—this won't get us bright-eyed and bushy-tailed in the morning,' she offered brightly, glancing at their empty coffee cups. She instantly wanted the words back, but too late now. Nathan had taken the hint and was on his feet.

Together they walked over to the lift. Together they rode up to the fifth floor—and never once did he ask her what she was doing tomorrow. It could have been, of course, that he was aware she would be under pressure from her father tomorrow. Or it could have been that he had no desire or intention to ask her to dinner only to have her father usurp him.

Either way they were at her door, the key in the lock, when Nathan glanced down at her. Last night he had kissed her. She wanted him to do so again. 'Goodnight,' said the contrary person inside of her who was determined she waited for no man's kisses.

She looked up then, and there was that look in Nathan's glance that said, What sort of a man do you think I am to let you go to bed unkissed? She gave in, she half smiled—he needed no further encouragement.

Last night he had lingeringly kissed her without otherwise touching her. Now he drew her gently to him. And it was bliss. Utter bliss!

'Goodnight,' he said softly, as he pulled back.

'G-goodnight,' she stammered, but her fingers were all thumbs suddenly and she couldn't get the door open.

Smoothly, Nathan took over. He opened up her door and switched on the light. She went inside, her heartbeats drumming. Joy of joys, Nathan stepped inside with her—and closed the door behind him.

'This is more private,' he said, and took her in his arms again.

Gently, he kissed her again and, as if starved, she willingly accepted his kiss. He broke his kiss to look down at her, as though to ascertain how she was feeling.

He must have seen that she was feeling never better because, moving further along the short hallway into her room, he once more took her into his arms. Nathan, Nathan… She wanted to cry his name, but was too choked to speak.

He raised his head to look down at her. 'All right?' he asked softly, as if afraid she really did have a hang-up when it came to such intimacies.

'All very all right,' she answered huskily. And loved him, loved his tender smile, and was all his when he gathered her to him and kissed her with a growing urgency.

She returned his kiss, felt his body against hers, and wanted to get even closer. But as that kiss ended and she opened her eyes the large alcove where the double bed was came into focus. And that was when she saw that the room staff had been in, and that the white and frothy very feminine nightdress that she had popped under her pillow that morning had been elegantly draped over the turned-back bedcovers, and suddenly everything seemed to her to be so much more extremely intimate—more extremely intimate than she was ready for.

'I—er…' she began, and Nathan's eyes followed her shaky glance to the bed.

And he was wonderful. She guessed many men would have endeavoured to push past that unseen barrier she was erecting, but not Nathan. Even though he probably knew that barrier was not insurmountable, he made no attempt to push through, but, letting her go, he teased lightly, 'Feet feeling the chill?'

'Oh, Nathan.' She laughed. But it was true, she was getting cold feet. 'Do you mind?'

He placed a light kiss to her parted lips. 'You must never, ever do anything that doesn't feel one hundred percent right to you,' he said, taking a step back.

'It—isn't—you,' she said chokily.

'I know that, my darling,' he replied tenderly.

And for just that she wanted to be back in his arms. But that bed, that nightdress, and the strictness of her childhood, the repressions of her adolescence, were not so easy to overcome.

'Goodnight, Nathan,' she bade him.

'Goodnight, sweetheart,' he answered, and went quickly, leaving her staring at the door. Was it any wonder that she loved him?

CHAPTER SEVEN

PHELIX lay awake for hours that night. How could she sleep? Nathan had called her his darling, had called her sweetheart, had intimated that he cared. Well, sort of. He cared for her—along with other females of his acquaintance, the sober part of her head reminded her. Yes, but he had also said that she was special.

She sighed, and turned over in her bed. None of which meant that he felt the same way about her that she felt about him, of course. But he had kissed her. Had held her close and kissed her—and had been understanding of whatever it was that held her back.

She loved him, she loved him, and she was not going home until Tuesday. Surely if it was true that he did care for her a little, if it was true that, for a little while anyway, she was his darling, then surely between now and Tuesday they would find space to spend a little time with each other?

Phelix turned over in her bed again as the unwanted thought pushed through the pleasantness of her world that she was making a giant something out of nothing. Was she presuming too much?

Doubts started to intrude. For heaven's sake, what had the poor man done but been gentle, been tender with her? He had spoken a few endearments that in some circles might be considered throwaway, and here she was imagining far more than he could ever be meaning.

Those doubts began to multiply. Nathan would be off to

his lawyers instigating their divorce sooner than *that* if he had the smallest notion of the way she had perceived his—his manner with her.

With doubts crowding in, sleep impossible, Phelix realised that if she wanted to continue to be friends with Nathan—and who said that friendship would extend beyond next Tuesday when she left for England, for goodness' sake?—then she had better be on her best guard to hide how even the smallest smile from him could affect her. If she went for a swim in the morning and Nathan was there…

At last from sheer weariness she dropped off into a light sleep. But it seemed no sooner had she closed her eyes than her telephone rang to wake her. She sat up, putting on the light and picking up the phone while at the same time checking her watch. Half past five!

'Hello?' she queried.

'I've booked you out on an early flight.' She heard her father's irascible tones. 'You'd better get your skates on.'

Phelix came quickly alert. She felt that during the past few days in foreign climes she had sloughed from her a little of her father's stifling pressure. She certainly was not ready to be manipulated by him at his merest whim.

'I haven't any plans to go anywhere,' she defied, certain as she was that this was just one more instance of him wanting control over her. She had opposed him last night when she'd agreed to have a drink with Nathan Mallory. This, without question, was her father's way of ensuring that she never had another drink with Nathan. Just as if she was some errant schoolgirl, and purely to keep her out of Nathan's sphere, he thought he could send her home! 'I've decided to stay here until next Tuesday as planned,' she stated unequivocally.

'If that's what you want to do that's fine by me,' he agreed pleasantly.

Something was wrong! This wasn't the father she knew and distrusted. 'Good,' she said. 'Thank you for waking me at five-thirty to have this little discussion.'

'Why, you cheeky b—!' That was more like him, but he managed to swallow down his ire. 'If you want to stay, that's up to you,' he went on. 'I'm sure Henry Scott will recover well and—'

Animosity with her father was forgotten on the instant. '*Henry*! What's the matter with Henry?' she asked urgently. 'Is he ill?'

'I took a phone call late last night—not so late in London. They're an hour behind us,' he inserted inconsequentially when she was more interested to know what was amiss with Henry than what the hour had been when her father's mistress had telephoned him. 'Apparently Henry collapsed yesterday and was carted off to hospital.'

'What's wrong with him?' she asked quickly.

'I didn't get more details, can't tell you which hospital, but it seems that he is asking for you.'

Oh, Henry, Henry. She swallowed down her feelings of panic. 'And you've arranged an early flight for me?'

'It was the first flight I could get. I thought you might want to go to him.'

'Thank you, Father,' Phelix said quietly, feeling a little amazed at his thoughtfulness—and also feeling a little ashamed of herself. He did have a good side, even if he did manage to keep it extremely well hidden.

'Think nothing of it,' he answered, and proceeded to give her details of the flight he had arranged for her.

Knowing that she had little time to spare after that phone call, Phelix took a hasty shower and then scurried around packing her case. She knew she would not be returning. By the sound of it Henry must have suffered a heart attack of some kind, and was asking for her. She must get to him with all speed.

But yet, with all the urgency of her actions, with most of her emotions taken up with fears for Henry, she could not help but think of Nathan.

She quite desperately felt that she wanted to perhaps write him a note and slip it under his door when she went. But against that was her fear that she was reading far more into their 'friendship' than he had intended. Wasn't he more likely to shrug, probably, hopefully, think It was nice knowing you, but add, It wasn't necessary for you to write.

She glanced at the phone as she was leaving. No, she decided firmly, when everything in her pulled her to have a quick word with him. Besides, it was too early to disturb him, and anyway…

Phelix was on her way when it dawned on her that while she had told Nathan a great deal about herself, he had told her little about himself. She knew she was highly vulnerable where he was concerned, and was then glad that she had not contacted him to say she was leaving.

What did she expect him to say, for goodness' sake, except—Bye! And that would have left her feeling an idiot, that she had disturbed him at that time in the morning. Well, at least she had spared herself that embarrassment.

Aware, though, of her vulnerability over him, Phelix used her years of bottling down her feelings to concentrate on the job in hand. Her first priority was to get to Henry.

It was a warm, sultry day when her plane landed in London. As she had no idea which hospital Henry was in, she decided to make a short stop at her office, where someone would obviously be able to tell her where Henry was to be found, and also the latest news on his progress, if any.

With fear clutching her heart at that last thought, Phelix raced to the Edward Bradbury building and straight up to the legal department. She was still in fact in the corridor, when the first person she saw was a fit and well looking—Henry Scott!

'Phelix!' he exclaimed in delight. 'I didn't expect you back today.' And, his eyes on her face, 'You look pale. Are you all right?'

Never better—now! 'I've—had a bit of a rush,' she replied, and as he looked at her, so she looked for any sign that he was unwell. 'I heard you were at death's door.' She was too shaken to hold it back.

'Oh, they don't want me up there just yet,' he answered breezily. And, as if where they were was much too public, 'Come into my office and tell me about your trip,' he invited.

'What happened with you?' she wanted to know the moment the door was closed and they'd moved over to a couple of chairs.

'Your father?' he guessed. 'He phoned you?'

This was no time to prevaricate. And in any event there was not much about her father and his 'little ways' that Henry did not know of. 'He's in Davos,' she informed him, and saw Henry's look of surprise.

'That snippet hasn't filtered down to me yet,' he stated, and they both knew that her father, probably suspecting that Henry would ring her to tell her that her father was on his way, had deliberately kept that information from him.

'He contacted me this morning to tell me you'd collapsed and been taken to hospital,' Phelix revealed. She felt it more important then to find out about the present state of Henry's health than to start getting angry that her father might have deliberately panicked her as some sort of reprisal for daring to defy him by meeting up with Nathan Mallory last night. 'You *did* collapse?' she wanted to know.

'Nothing too dramatic...' Henry began, and she *was* panicked.

'What happened?' she asked swiftly.

'Nothing other than the fact I had a forgetful moment in my old age and, when it's become second nature to me over the years, I somehow managed to mistime my insulin shot.'

'Insul... You're a diabetic?' she asked, startled.

'True.'

'I didn't know!' she protested.

'There's no reason why you should know. It's well under control—normally.'

'But not yesterday?'

'An oversight on my part. It won't happen again.'

'You blacked out?'

'It was a bit of a pantomime.' He made light of it. 'I went shopping instead of having lunch—and the next I know I'm coming round in hospital. They'd obviously done a sugar test when I stayed unconscious, taken the appropriate action—and kept me there until they considered I was well enough to leave.'

'Should you be here? Shouldn't you be resting?'

'Now, don't get in a stew, there's a good girl,' he said warmly, his tone fatherly. 'I'm absolutely fine. It was a one-off.'

She looked at him and realised he did not want any fuss, that he wanted to play it lightly. 'The way I heard it, you were asking for me,' she commented, seemingly off-handedly.

'Who else would I call for as I came out of it,' he teased, 'but my very good friend, Phelix?'

She smiled, feeling heartily relieved that while his collapse had been serious he had been quickly attended to. It passed through her mind to wonder if her father knew far more about Henry's collapse than he had told her. Most probably, most certainly, she realised, he did.

But, having ascertained that Henry had suffered no permanent damage, there was something more important on her mind just then than that her father had manipulated her out of one country and away from a man he did not want her to have anything to do with and into another country.

'You've been a very good friend to me too, Henry, haven't you?' she asked.

'Oh, my, you're looking serious,' he said lightly, noncommittal until he found on what she was meaning.

Phelix knew then that, having always guarded over her, he

vas unlikely to admit anything that he considered was likely o cause her the smallest distress. Which meant that she was oing to have to bring what was in her mind out into the open.

'You know the name of the man I married, don't you, Henry?' he asked, and, knowing that he would not lie to her, waited.

And, having weighed up all the pros and cons, 'I've always nown,' he admitted. 'From day two.'

'You went to the register office?'

'Don't be cross, Phelix,' Henry soothed, when she was not t all cross with him. 'You were so very upset, and while I ould do little about what had taken place, I'd have been failing n my duty to your mother if I hadn't checked who the man was nd what consequences, if any, might be in store for you.'

'Oh, Henry,' she said softly, and asked then what she upposed she had over the years grown to know, 'You—loved ny mother, didn't you?'

Henry looked from her briefly, but turned back to answer uietly, 'Felicity was a saint.' Going on to reveal, 'It was my sinerest hope that I might one day be able to ask her to marry me.'

Phelix felt tears prick her eyes. Strangely, she was not startled o hear what Henry had just said. It was just painful that, when er mother could have had a much better life with Henry, for her hild's sake, she had stayed with her mean, abusive husband.

'Oh, dear, dear, Henry,' Phelix murmured. 'You knew she ad a rough time with my father?'

'I would only have made matters worse had I gone to sort im out,' he admitted.

'You stayed on here, working for him?'

'I didn't want to. I turned down several better offers. But if 'd given up my work here, I would also have given up the hance to do any small service I could for Felicity. And,' he pened up, 'when Felicity was taken from me—even though I new she was not mine…'

'You stayed on here—for me?' Phelix guessed.

'I could see you might go the same subjugated way your mother went. I wasn't having that. Not that I needed to,' Henry said with a smile. 'I think you started to find yourself on the day you married Nathan Mallory.'

'And you encouraged me—every step of the way.'

'It was always there in you.'

'Just needed a little nurturing?' she offered lightly.

'Had things gone as I wanted, you'd have been my daughter—my stepdaughter,' he qualified. 'Naturally I encouraged you.'

Phelix knew he would have made a superb stepfather, and felt quite choked for the moment. But he had always looked out for her anyway. Inwardly she mourned for the life her mother might have had, for what might have been. But, getting herself back together, she asked that which had to be asked, 'Was it you who sent that note to Nathan Mallory?'

'What note would that be?'

'You're hedging,' Phelix accused. 'I *know* it was you.' And she nudged when he did not answer. 'Eight years ago? Your friend Oscar Livingstone—remember?'

'Good heavens!'

'Exactly. When I told you of the shameful way Nathan had been treated you had him checked out and then you contacted Mr Livingstone. Following on from your conversation with him, you sent a note by messenger to Nathan suggesting he phone him.'

'Good heavens!' Henry exclaimed again. 'I knew you were bright, but how on earth did you work that out?'

'I didn't. I had help. Nathan Mallory is in Davos. We got talking...' Her voice faded. She remembered Nathan's strong arms about her, recalled his wonderful kisses...

'Nathan Mallory worked it out?' Henry did not seem surprised to hear that Nathan had been in Switzerland at the same time as her. 'How come?' he asked.

'Um—as I said, we got talking. I told him about you coming

› my home the day after the wedding and how I'd told you ev-
:ything but the name of the man I married. I also happened to
ıy how you seemed to know everyone, and Nathan worked it
ut from there.'

'How did you get on with him?' Henry asked.

Phelix felt herself blushing. 'Very well,' she answered.
.dding quickly, 'We had dinner one night and I was foolish
ıough to mention it to my father when he phoned.'

'I bet he caught the first plane out,' Henry said cheerfully.

And Phelix had to laugh. 'Do you know, Henry, I think you
ave a streak of wickedness in you?'

'And all these years I've been trying to keep it hidden.'

Phelix got up from her chair, and when he stood up too, she
'ent over to him. 'Thank you so very much for saving Nathan
om losing everything,' she said softly, and stretched up and
issed him.

'He's more than proved himself worthy of saving,' he
ıswered sincerely. And, musing aloud, 'Do you think I should
y to contact your father to tell him to stop worrying about me?'

'You *are* wicked!' Phelix branded him, and they both smiled.

She went to her office after leaving him, but was all of a
ıdden overcome by such a feeling of restlessness that she
›und it impossible to settle. She checked through to see if there
as anything urgent pending. And then, telling herself that she
'asn't expected in her office until next Wednesday, she, for
›out the first time in her working career, turned her back on
.e diligence of her nature, phoned through to tell Henry where
ıe was going, and went home.

Home was quiet without Grace there. And to rattle around
the cold mausoleum of her home did absolutely nothing to
ıse her restless feelings.

She unpacked her case, threw some laundry in the washing
ıachine and, time hanging heavily, wondered if perhaps she
ɔuld not have been better to have stayed at work.

Though in her heart she knew what was wrong with her was more a restlessness of spirit than a restlessness because she had nothing to do. Less than twenty-four hours ago Nathan had kissed her…

While Phelix was glad that Henry had quickly recovered, she began to see it as fact that her father, with his 'We'll see about that,' had totally and without the smallest compunction used Henry's temporary indisposition to remove her from Nathan Mallory's orbit.

And she had fallen for it! He had left it until the last minute to tell her of her flight. Not that she could regret dashing home to check on Henry the way she had, but oh, how she longed, positively ached, to be back where she might see Nathan again. They had been staying in the same hotel, for goodness' sake. Surely she would…

Phelix spent the next half-hour going around in mental circles. With her whole physical being she wanted to be back in Davos. With the whole of her logical thinking brain she knew her small 'dalliance' with Nathan was over. Just as she knew she had been right to leave as she had without letting him know. Her face burned with the thought of the idiot she would have made of herself had she slipped any kind of a note beneath his door.

It was over, finished. Possibly, from his point of view, never begun. Good grief—he would be amazed if he thought she had read anything more into his kisses than, for him, a small pleasure of the moment. Think of something else, do!

In an endeavour to do that very thing, Phelix went to the kitchen where Grace kept a board with a list of phone numbers. And in the next minute she was speaking to Grace's friend Midge.

'I wondered if you'd heard from Grace recently?' Phelix began, after saying who she was.

'Grace is here now. Just a minute.'

And within that minute Grace was on the line. 'You're back?' she asked.

'Came back today,' Phelix replied, and asked, 'What happened, Grace?'

'I've been cooking him his favourite steak and kidney for umpteen years now—and suddenly he decides I'm not making it right!' Grace exclaimed indignantly.

'You had words?'

'The fur flew!' Grace laughed.

'You're obviously feeling better about it now.'

'I'm still not coming back, if that's what you're asking.'

'It isn't,' Phelix replied. 'I just wanted to make sure that you're all right?'

'I'm fine. I'm staying with Midge for a short while, while I consider my options. But actually, Phelix, and don't take it personally, but it's something of a relief to be out of that house.'

Phelix did not take it personally. She was having the same sort of feelings herself. She stayed chatting to Grace for quite some time, and ended the conversation by asking Grace to let her know if she needed help of any sort or in any way. She made a mental note to include a hefty bonus in Grace's salary and to try to keep in touch, and rang off, wishing that she, like Grace, could just pack her cases and be off.

She admitted that the idea had tremendous appeal, but supposed she had better hang around until a new housekeeper had been found and installed. She— A distant rumble of thunder interrupted her thoughts. A thunderstorm had been threatening for some while.

The air stayed sultry, but to Phelix's relief the storm stayed in the distance. She went to bed that night with the threat of a thunderstorm miles away from her mind. Thoughts of Nathan Mallory had taken precedence. He was her one love. She, as far as he was concerned, she did not doubt, was one of many—and love didn't come into it.

The air was still heavy when she got up the next morning. It needed a thunderstorm to clear it, but she would far rather be in Switzerland when at last the storm broke. Switzerland and Nathan were back with her.

She attempted matters practical. She had spent time yesterday clearing up a backlog of dishwashing that her father had not deigned to clean his hands with. That Saturday morning Phelix set about putting the house in some sort of order.

Having vacuumed and polished, with Nathan her companion the whole while, Phelix went out for fresh milk and a few other oddments. Her appetite had gone, but she would try and find something tempting to eat.

By eight o'clock that night, having munched her way through a salad, finishing off with a banana, Phelix went up to her room to shower. The air was oppressive, and she knew if she did not take her shower now there was no way she was going to do so once the storm that had been threatening well and truly broke.

She felt marginally refreshed after her shower, but was wide awake. In any event, it was much too early to go to bed.

Doubting that she would sleep anyway, she slipped into a lightweight black silk leisure suit. It was something she seldom wore, but it was too hot for anything heavier. But with no one else in the house, she might as well take a book to the drawing room sofa.

By ten o'clock she knew it was a ridiculous idea. She was going to have to do something about Nathan Mallory. He was interfering with her head big time.

Determined to stick it out until eleven, Phelix again tried to get interested in her book—only this time for a violent clap of thunder to tear her concentration to shreds. Feeling hot and clammy, she strove to keep calm—but nearly jumped out of her skin when at that precise moment the doorbell sounded.

She went swiftly from the drawing room to the front door, and as another clap of thunder rent the air she forgot entirely her more normal caution to check through the spyhole to see who was there before opening the door, and urgently pulled it back.

Shock made her momentarily dumb. 'Nathan!' she gasped when she had her breath back, still half ready to believe that she was imagining that he stood there. A fork of lightning lit the sky. 'Come in!' she invited hastily. 'You'll get soaked out there!'

Phelix took a shaky breath as—tall, superb, and so loved—Nathan Mallory stepped over the threshold. She quickly closed the door, her heart hammering to see him again so amazingly unexpectedly, so wonderfully unexpectedly, as she strove hard to find some sense of normality. What was he doing here? She had imagined him in Switzerland. He should *be* in Switzerland!

'What brings you to this neck of the woods?' she asked lightly, while trying to keep a lid on her soaring excitement. He wasn't here to see her father. Indeed, she would have thought that he would never want to set foot inside her home again after the last time. But he *was* here! So Nathan, having left Switzerland for some reason, *must* have come to see her!

'My car broke down nearby,' he replied, but there was such a look in his warm grey eyes that she knew he was lying.

'Try again?' she invited. 'No car of yours would ever dream of breaking down.'

He grinned, and she loved him. 'I was bored,' he offered.

She looked him over. Dark-haired, mind-blowingly impressive—and wearing an immaculate suit, collar and tie. 'All dressed up and nowhere to go?' she queried.

'I took her home,' he admitted, adding quickly, 'Didn't stay.'

Phelix did not know which she was first—jealous that he had taken out some other woman, or delighted that he had been bored with the other woman's company. Then she became conscious of her thin trousers and top, became aware that Nathan was now flicking his glance over her the way she had flicked her glance over him. And she just knew, as his eyes traced briefly over her breasts, that he knew she was not wearing underwear.

'It was hot!' she said, in a rush to explain her thin attire—and bang went the air of sophistication she was trying to achieve.

'Oh, love,' he murmured.

But she was feeling awkward and vulnerable, and was not waiting for anything else he might add. 'Coffee?' she offered jerkily. 'Shall I make you some coffee?'

Nathan looked at her tenderly, every bit as if he knew how she was feeling. 'I'd love some coffee,' he accepted quietly.

Trying to not break out into a sprint, Phelix went quickly along the hall. 'If you'd like to wait in here?' She put her best hostess hat on at the open drawing room door.

'Can I help?' he offered.

'No,' she refused lightly. 'It will only take me a couple of minutes.'

She left him at the drawing room door and went quickly to the kitchen. She was glad she had offered him coffee, glad he had accepted, but knew that she must put in some very hard work in those couple of coffee-making minutes to try and get herself back to one piece again.

And then abruptly there was an almighty crack of thunder and she saw her mother's face, saw her pleading with her father, and on the heels of that first crack another horrendous clap—it must have been directly overhead. The lights flickered and went out, and she thought she might have cried out. But even as she was striving to hold herself together the lights came on again, and Nathan was there.

He placed his hands on her shoulders and turned her to him, his arms coming round her to hold her safe as he pulled her to him. 'Still bad?' he asked softly, understanding.

She nodded into his shoulder. She felt safe with him. 'I'm all right now,' she said shakily, drawing back to look at him, and making to move out of his hold.

'Don't be a spoilsport,' he teased gently. 'You know how much I enjoy having you in my arms.'

'Oh, Nathan,' she wailed, but, as perhaps he had hoped, he had drawn a smile from her. 'Coffee,' she said determinedly, and would, she thought, have found the strength to have pulled out of his arms. But then he bent down and gently kissed her—and she had no strength to do anything after that.

'I'm not really interested in coffee,' he commented.

There was that look in his eyes that said he was interested in her, but she felt so mixed up just then she was not at all sure that she was reading the signals correctly.

'And—um—you haven't truly broken down in your car?' She strove for some clarification.

Nathan shook his head. 'I parked it on the side of your drive. I wanted to see you, Phelix,' he added softly.

Oh, Nathan! Her spine was beginning to melt. 'That's—um—nice,' she managed, and he laughed lightly in delight with her.

'You can do better than that,' he suggested.

And, looking up into his tender grey eyes, she knew that she could. She stretched up and kissed his cheek, and held him close. 'Better?' she asked, pulling away, but only to feel his arms about her tighten before she could move too far.

'Hmm—I think I should warn you—there's a chance we could be getting into serious territory here,' Nathan, his hold still firm, thought to mention.

Phelix looked at him—and needed help. 'I'm not sure how I feel about that,' she replied honestly, and didn't think she liked it when Nathan relaxed his hold on her and seemed about to step back. 'But that doesn't mean I wouldn't like to—er—um…'

'Do a little research?'

Phelix got cold feet again. 'I'll make that coffee,' she said firmly, and would have been the one to step away, only he held her steady.

'There's no call to be totally unfriendly,' he rebuked her. 'Why not stay just where you are and give me one good reason why you didn't let me know you were doing a flit?'

From Switzerland, obviously. She should have let him know. *Now*, with Nathan here, she felt she should have done so. 'I

wanted to let you know, but…' She just couldn't tell him tha
she had not done so because she had not wanted to presume o
their friendship—or whatever it was.

'But you preferred me to find out from your father?'

'Did he tell you I'd…?'

'He came to the hotel to settle your hotel bill, so he said. Bu
since I'm sure you would have settled it yourself, to all purpose
and effect he came and waited until he saw me, in order to le
me know how you'd phoned him to ask him to arrange for yo
to catch the first flight you could.'

'It—wasn't quite like that,' she confessed. She loved th
way Nathan was holding her. 'Um…' She tried to get he
thoughts together.

'You didn't leave because you thought I'd come on to
heavy when I kissed you the way I did?' he queried seriously

And she stared at him, startled, amazed that he should hav
thought such a thing. There seemed to her then only one wa
to show just how wrong he had been if he'd thought that.

Raising her head, she stretched up and, ignoring his chee
this time, she touched her lips to his. No brief meeting of lips
she kissed him long and lingeringly. She had to admit to feelin
a shade flushed when she pulled back from him.

Nathan looked steadily into her wide green eyes. 'I'm con
vinced,' he said softly, and then proceeded to take over fron
where he had left off on Thursday evening.

Somehow or other his jacket and tie were hanging on th
back of a chair, and Phelix felt the warmth of his chest burnin
into her through her thin covering when, holding her firmly i
his arms, his lips met hers, seeking and finding a response.

'You're beautiful, my darling,' he breathed as their kis
broke and he gazed tenderly down at her. And as she thrille
to his endearment, rejoiced that Nathan the man she love
thought her beautiful, he kissed her again.

Her arms went up and around him. He was warm and won

derful and she was enchanted to be in his arms, to be kissed and held by him.

Then suddenly she was not so sure. She loved him. She knew that she always would. But as his warm seeking hands found their way beneath her thin top, something she had no control of seemed to be tripping her up.

She felt his hands on the bare skin of her back, caressing upward—proof there if needed, when there was no bra to hinder his caresses, that she had nothing else on.

Nathan kissed her again, a long enchanting kiss, and she started to breathe a little more easily. But then those seeking hands began to search beneath her top around to the front of her—and she abruptly jerked back, taking a step away from him. His hands fell from her.

'I'm s-sorry,' she apologised, feeling uptight again, embarrassed and…

'You've nothing to be sorry for,' Nathan assured her calmly, his eyes on her as if reading her face.

'You'll think I'm a t-tease, or something,' she stammered.

'Don't you think I know you better than that?' he asked quietly.

There was perhaps about a yard now separating them. 'Do you know me?' she asked. 'It's less than a week since we met.'

'I've been married to you for eight years, remember?' he queried, his mouth quirking up at the corners as he tried to get a smile from her. 'And, while there's a lot more we need to know about each other, I know that you're good, you're kind, and that you're as honest as the day. I think that's a very good start, don't you?'

A start to what? Her heart was pounding madly. 'I—wanted to leave a note to tell you where I'd gone, but—but I didn't want you to think…' Her voice failed her.

'I think you should learn to trust your instincts more than you do,' Nathan offered quietly.

'You—do?'

'While keeping a natural caution,' he qualified.

And she smiled, and wanted to kiss him, but did not dare risk it. She did not know what was wrong with her, but there was some insurmountable barrier that, no matter how much she loved him, she could not get through.

'M-my father received word that Henry had collapsed—he, my father, arranged for me to get home quickly,' she explained in a rush.

'You're too far away over there,' Nathan commented, but made no move to come any closer.

Trust your instincts, he had said. Phelix took a deep breath and moved close to him. Still he did not touch her. She stretched out her hands and placed them on his waist.

'What's wrong with me?' she asked.

Nathan looked deeply into her eyes. 'Sweet darling,' he murmured lightly, 'with so much right with you, I'd be a little scared of you if there wasn't something just a tiny bit out of kilter.'

'I don't believe you've ever been scared of anything,' she offered, but as lightly, and had to smile.

She guessed Nathan took that as an encouraging smile, because, although he made no move to kiss her again, he caught her to him in a loose hold and instructed, 'So relax, and tell me how Henry is. Was it a heart attack?'

She did relax, and felt good. 'That's what I thought too. I didn't know which hospital he'd been taken to, so I detoured to the office first—and there to my astonishment, looking fit and well, was Henry himself.'

'Your father panicked you for the pure hell of it?'

'Not exactly. Henry had collapsed and had been taken to hospital. But it wasn't his heart—he'd forgotten his insulin shot. I'd no idea he was a diabetic!'

'Poor Phelix,' Nathan sympathised.

'Poor Henry,' she countered, but then smiled broadly as she told Nathan, 'You were right. It was Henry who sent you that note.'

Nathan smiled too. 'After he'd contacted Oscar Livingstone on my behalf,' he filled in. 'You told him of my suspicions?'

'I had to. He wondered how I'd worked it out—I said I had help.'

'I'll set up a meeting with him,' Nathan said, as she had perhaps known that he would.

She looked at him then, and as she looked at him she seemed to read something in his eyes—as if he was quietly waiting—though what for she had not a clue. But she was suddenly filled with so much love for him that she could hardly bear it.

'I want to kiss you,' somebody else in charge of her said huskily.

Nathan's expression did not change. 'If that is what you want to do, Phelix,' he replied softly, 'I have to tell you that I have absolutely no objection.'

'Oh, Nathan,' she cried. 'What if I get cold feet again?'

For answer, he smiled gently. 'I'm a big boy. I'll cope,' he said.

She looked from his eyes to his warm superb mouth, and all at once Nathan was meeting her halfway. And it was such a joy to be held warm and safe and close up to his heart again.

'All right?' he questioned when their kiss broke.

'May I have another?'

He laughed lightly. No pressure. 'I think we can manage that,' he agreed, and suddenly she was in seventh heaven again, as they exchanged wonderful long and sometimes short kisses.

She placed her arms up and over his shoulders and he held her to him, not attempting to touch her more intimately. Though she was aware, when a moment later their lips met again, that his kisses were growing more and more passionate.

A fire started to burn in her for him. She welcomed it, and, barely being aware of what she was doing, she pressed herself to him.

But gently he was easing her a little bit away from him, and as that kiss broke, 'Darling, Phelix,' he said softly, 'I love you so much, but…'

Colour flared instantly to her face. He loved her! Joy such as she had never known broke in her. She kissed him, her own passion soaring. Nathan loved her. It was all she wanted to hear. And, more than that, with those words 'I love you so much' it seemed as if every one of those insurmountable barriers she had subconsciously put up had on that moment collapsed, disappeared without trace.

That was, there was still one barrier there, in that she wanted to tell Nathan that she loved him in return, but shyness seemed to freeze the words to her tongue.

Which made it the biggest mystery to her that, as their kiss ended and they looked at each other, and to her heightened senses it seemed as though for his sanity's sake Nathan might put her away from him, she found her tongue to urgently tell him, 'Nathan, I w-want to make love with you.'

He halted, and looked at her as if he could hardly believe his ears. 'You want to make love?' he asked, as if checking his hearing.

'Yes,' she replied without hesitation. She might be a little red about the ears, but her answer was honest.

Nathan looked deeply into her eyes, and then drew her to him. And the next time he kissed her there was more passion there, and she rejoiced in that passion. He held her close, and then it was that his hands began to caress her back, began to find their way beneath her thin silk top.

He broke that kiss to pull a little way away from her, but his hands were still beneath her top as, unhurriedly, his long sensitive fingers caressed their way to the front of her.

Phelix held her breath in exquisite torture as his hands held her ribcage. 'You're sure?' he asked quietly.

She was feeling very much on uncharted ground, but, 'I'm sure,' she answered huskily—and felt the most sublime pleasure when his hands moved upwards and his sensitive fingers captured her love-swollen breasts, his eyes on hers the whole of the time.

'You're still sure?' he asked.

This was new territory for her. It was the first time she had wanted any man. But Nathan was not just any man, he was the man she loved—her husband. And she adored his touch.

She swallowed on a knot of emotion, but was unwavering when she replied, 'I was never more certain.'

'You darling,' Nathan breathed. 'My brave darling.' And with that, obviously deciding to not make love to her in the kitchen, he gathered her up in his strong arms and strode from the kitchen with her towards the stairs.

'I'm heavier than I used to be,' was the only protest Phelix made as he carried her up the stairs.

'Delightfully so,' he replied, pausing to bend and kiss her—and then moving on to unerringly find the bedroom where they had last lain together.

But this time it was different. This time she was no immature teenager in need of comfort from the storm. This time she was a warm, vibrant and wanting woman!

The only light in the room came from the bedside lamp that Nathan switched on. They kissed and held, and Nathan let go of her briefly to divest himself of his shirt, and Phelix, her heart full, could only wonder at the splendour of him.

She stretched out a hand to his broad naked chest and marvelled at this intimacy they shared. He looked warmly at her, took her hand to his mouth and kissed it, and then drew her closer to him.

The warmth of his uncovered chest burned into her through her thin top. She loved him so. She was his whenever he chose. Though when he made to remove her top, Phelix discovered that she still had a few inhibitions remaining.

She caught a hold of his wrists to stop him. 'I—can't,' she said jerkily, nervously.

Nathan instantly stilled. 'You can't—make love?' he asked, his voice quiet, controlled, with not an atom of anger with her in evidence.

She shook her head, feeling gauche and awkward suddenly. 'The light,' she explained huskily. And adored him when he straight away seemed to understand that she was already making giant leaps from the repression that had held her in a merciless grip, but that she was not yet ready to stand naked before him in full view in the lamplight.

'Sweet love,' he said softly, kissed her gently, and then bent to put out the light.

'Oh, Nathan,' she whispered, and was in an enchanted land she had never known as he kissed and caressed her and kissed her. And as he again went to remove her top, she did what she could to help him.

And then they were standing naked together, and as he kissed and caressed her breasts, taking a hardened peak into his mouth, Phelix was no longer thinking, only feeling.

Nathan held her close, and as Phelix felt his all maleness against her, so she started to tremble. 'You're doing magnificently, my darling,' he soothed, feeling her trembling body against him, and he moved with her to lie down on her bed and—she was enraptured.

They kissed, their legs entwined, and she wanted to touch him, to stroke him all over—but, a private person herself, she had no idea what was and what was not acceptable.

'Help me to know what to do?' she pleaded softly.

'Oh, darling innocent,' Nathan crooned, feeling her trembling still as he held her. 'Do whatever feels right to you.' And again he kissed her, kissed her lips, her eyes, her throat, and while she could barely breathe from the ecstasy of his tenderness, he kissed her breasts, their pink tips—and she rejoiced in his kisses.

And as desire for him soared in her, so she began to feel liberated. She touched and caressed his nipples, her arms going round him, and they clung to each other. Her fingers played over his back and she marvelled at the wonderful exquisite feel of him.

Nathan came to half lie over her, and she felt his hands on her naked behind, pulling her to him. And knew joy unfettered when, tracing her hands down his back, she was able to likewise hold his superb behind.

Unrestrained, they pressed into each other. But then, when Phelix was feeling quite dizzy with delight, Nathan moved a little away from her and, while still tenderly kissing her, his caressing hands travelled down over her breasts and down to her belly.

Then all at once, as his sensitive touch was gently exploring further, Phelix knew as she thrilled to his touch that they had reached a point of no return. Nor did she want to return. Making love with Nathan was beyond anything she had ever known.

She loved him, and as he wanted her so she wanted him. Though when his exploring fingers became even more intimate, and her breath caught, she could not hold in a small cry of hesitancy.

Nathan stilled. 'Problem?' he queried, as if suspecting he might have suddenly come up against a last minute brick wall of her inhibitions.

And she, fearing he might stop, quickly found her voice to tell him, 'Just a momentary blip of—um—shyness.' She kissed him then, pressing herself hard against him as passionately as she knew, in the hope that he would know from that that she would just about die if he went and left her wanting him like this.

'My sweet love,' he breathed, and as passion between them flared out of control, and as if he knew she would wait no longer, he came to lie over her and eased himself between her parted thighs. 'I love you, sweet darling,' he murmured, and she—she loved him so, and joyously welcomed him.

CHAPTER EIGHT

IT FELT incredible to Phelix to awake at dawn in the arms of the man she loved. Joy awoke within her as she recalled Nathan's utter tenderness with her. She had awoken during the night but, as if somehow anything she might say might take away the sublime magic, she had stayed still and silent—and just rejoiced to have Nathan so near.

He had told her he loved her—she wanted to pinch herself in case it was just a wonderful dream. But it was no dream. She could feel the heat of his body next to hers beneath the sheet their only covering on such a warm night.

Oddly, when she had so wanted to tell him of her own feelings, of how she loved him in return, she had felt too shy to voice those words that were in the very heart of her, those words that were a stranger to her.

Her shyness was totally ridiculous, she knew, when she considered the absolute freedom she and Nathan had shared with each other. The absolute, enrapturing freedom.

But Nathan knew what she had been too shy to tell him. He must know, surely?

Oh, Nathan. They had made love—sublime, perfect, incredible love. Her heart felt full as she recalled the exquisitely tender way he had been with her. Never had she thought a man could be so gentle, so caring of her discomfort when slowly unhurriedly, taking time because of her untried body, he had lovingly taken her virginity.

A small sigh involuntarily escaped her—and her joy soared. Nathan was awake too, and had heard the sound.

'Good morning, Mrs Mallory,' he breathed softly.

'Oh, Nathan.' She turned, her body happily colliding with his. Thrilled by his words, she moved her head to look at him, and warm colour rushed to her face.

'You can still blush?' he teased softly, his grey gaze warm on her.

Again she felt the need to tell him that she loved him, but again shyness kept the words unsaid.

'Er—good morning, Mr Mallory,' she answered, and loved and wanted him when he bent to her and kissed her. 'Oh,' she sighed, and when he pulled her close up to him, she knew that as she had instantly desired him, so Nathan instantly wanted her.

He kissed her again, one arm holding her, one hand caressing her right shoulder. And again they kissed, passion soaring, that hand leaving her shoulder to caress her breast, until suddenly Nathan pulled back from her.

'Is it too soon for you?' he asked, releasing her breast, holding her waist and moving fractionally away, as though striving to turn the temperature down.

For a moment she was unsure what he meant. But, recalling his care of her last night, she suddenly realised that he must be thinking that perhaps her newly tested body might need to recover.

'I want you,' she said simply, and kissed him, and held his warm fantastic-to-the-touch hip so he should come in close again.

He smiled at her, but did not come any closer. 'I'm glad,' he said, and gently kissed her.

But whether he would have made love with her then or not she did not know. What she did know was that in the next second the mood was heartbreakingly shattered, spoilt, abruptly fractured beyond repair, when—with a crack of thunder that sounded as if the heavens had split in two—simultaneously, paralysingly, her father came charging into her bedroom!

Shock made her world spin! Having been so completely enraptured by Nathan that, remarkably, she had been entirely unaware of the gathering storm, she had been unaware too that her father had returned from Switzerland!

Feeling dizzy from being so cruelly torn out from the bliss she had been sharing with Nathan, Phelix stared at her father, completely astounded that with that crack of thunder he had come roaring in.

'I knew it!' he bellowed, his face contorted with rage, and, venting his apoplectic wrath on her bed companion, 'That's your car parked on my drive, Mallory! Well, *bloody well* move it—and yourself with it!'

The scene was ugly. Desire died an instant death. No way could it have survived. Surprisingly, as Phelix started to surface from being stupefied, she felt no shame that her father should have found her in bed with Nathan. What did shame her was that he could speak to Nathan the way he did.

'I'm not here at your invitation,' Nathan replied calmly, taking his arms from her and sitting up. Phelix, pulling the bedsheet close up to her, sat up too.

'Too bloody right you're not!' Edward Bradbury shouted. 'Nor likely to be! This is my house and I say who enters it!' he spluttered—and as thunder and lightning joined in the bedlam and her father's face contorted again, so Phelix was once more back in the night when her mother had died. Lightning forked, and again she saw her father's face twisted and evil as he had set about doing her mother harm.

Phelix strove hard not to flinch as her father continued to shout, but she felt the colour drain from her as nausea invaded. From experience she knew she had to appear calm, but it took a tremendous effort and years of self-training to hide just how sick she felt inside.

Outwardly unflustered, she became vaguely aware of Nathan leaving her bed and getting into his clothes. But, with her insides already churning, she had to endure a feeling of humiliation too that, with her father still yelling—pointless to try and argue with him—Nathan should find himself a part of the vile scene. It mortified her that because of her he had become embroiled in such ugly unpleasantness.

Feeling shamed and flattened, she found the two awful scenes alternating in her head: flashes of her father's physical assault on her mother, and his present verbal assault on the man she loved.

She saw Nathan's jaw clench, saw his hands bunch, and had an idea, as her father continued to scream abuse at him to take himself off his premises, that Nathan was having a hard time holding down on the urge to silence the older man with his fists. But her father, his face malevolent as it had been that terrible night, was still roaring at him to get out when Nathan looked across at her, at her ashen face.

'Phelix.' He said her name, which brought her away from that night. But what Nathan would have added she did not wait to hear.

She could not take it. At any moment now her father's language would ripen, and on top of this, she knew she just would not be able to bear the degrading ignominy of it.

'Go, Nathan,' she pleaded, pulling the bedsheet defensively up and around her. 'Please go,' she begged.

His eyes followed her movements with the sheet and he hesitated, seemed torn. 'I'm not leaving you alone with this madman. He—'

'Do as she says! Clear off before I call the police!' Edward Bradbury erupted.

Nathan ignored him. 'Phelix, you—'

'It's better if you go.' She interrupted him this time, half hoping that he would say, Come with me. But he did not say that, though with her father still proving that his lung power had not diminished over the years, he would have had a job making himself heard. 'He'll calm down once you've gone,' she promised.

Nathan did not look convinced, but asked, in the space provided when her father paused for breath, 'I'm making things worse by staying?'

'I know it,' she answered. And, as Nathan still seemed to be having a mental struggle within himself, 'Please go,' she urged. 'Please.'

Nathan still did not look entirely convinced but, as if conceding that she must know her father and his rages far better than him, asked, 'You'll be all right if I leave?'

Phelix nodded, wanting him gone before her father should mortify her further by resorting to the kind of language he used when his outrage spilled over into foul mouthed obscenity.

'I'm used to him. He'll calm down soon,' she said—hoped.

And wanted to weep when, after long moments of studying her calm expression, despite her insides being all of a heap, Nathan, with her father on his heels, did as she asked and left the room.

In a kind of numb shock she heard them going down the stairs, heard another altercation break out when Nathan detoured to the kitchen for his jacket, tie and car keys. It was still going on when she heard the slam of a car door—and then heard Nathan's car roar down the drive.

Tears came then. Floods of them. Phelix rushed from her room to her bathroom and locked herself in. The storm was still going on overhead as she stood under the shower—she barely noticed.

Last night with Nathan had been magical. Look at it now! In ruins! Smithereens! It wasn't Nathan's fault. Dear God, he had been wonderful. It was her father. He had spoilt it as he spoilt everything else.

She guessed he would come upstairs, possibly come into her room again to turn his vitriol on her. But the shower was her sanctuary. She knew she would not be disturbed.

But after some while she knew that, since she could not stay in the bathroom all day, she had better get dressed and decide what she was going to do. Because it went without saying that this was the end as far as she and her father were concerned.

Drying her eyes, she took a grim if shaky breath and, leaving her bathroom, went into her bedroom. The bed seemed to suddenly dominate it. Feeling compelled, she gave in to a moment of weakness and went and sat on the edge of her bed, on the side where Nathan had lain. She picked up his pillow and held it to the side of her face, her heart crying out for him.

Humiliation deep and bitter racked her that Nathan had had to put up with her father haranguing him. She did not know how she would ever face Nathan again, or if indeed he would want to see her again after that appalling scene. She'd like to bet that in all his home life he had never ever witnessed or been forced to be part of anything that was a quarter as vile as the treatment her father had dealt him.

Swallowing back fresh tears, determined to not cry again, Phelix left the bed and got dressed with her head in a turmoil.

First things first, she decided. But what came first? She was striving to think logically, though with that scene bouncing back at her all the time she was finding logical thinking difficult to hang on to.

But, making a start, she stripped her bed and went and put the sheets and pillowcases in the washing machine. The phone rang—her father answered it before she could get from the laundry room to the kitchen phone. She made a dive for it anyway, but her father must have had the briefest call on record, because as she picked it up all she heard was the sound of the dialling tone. He had obviously ended the call before it had begun.

Her spirits lifted momentarily—had that been Nathan?

Hoping that the caller might have been Nathan, she realised she might be able to find his number by dialling one four seven one. But before she had the chance the phone rang again, cancelling out the previous number. Her father had snatched up the receiver at the same time, but since the call was for him, from Anna Fry, Phelix had no interest in the call and replaced the receiver.

Her spirits zoomed down to zero. If the previous call had been Nathan her father would deny it. No two ways about it, he would not have taken a message for her. It would be pointless to ask him. Not that she felt inclined to ever speak to her father again.

She went back up the stairs to fold her bedding and to pack as many of her belongings as she could. Anything she hadn't got she would do without or collect at a later date. For now she was doing what she should have done years ago—she was leaving.

Phelix took one of her two suitcases and a holdall out to her car, and went back to her room for the other one and a bag containing toiletries and bits and pieces.

She had no mind to see her father, but, supposing his girlfriend's call would have calmed him down, Phelix did not shrink from going to see him. Taking her case with her, and with a car coat over her arm, she went along the hall to the drawing room.

He looked up when she went in, his mouth thinning to an even tighter narrow line when he saw she was carrying a suitcase. She did not wait for him to start, but plunged straight in.

'You'd better set about finding a new housekeeper. I've had a word with Grace; she isn't coming back—and I'm leaving.'

'You don't think for a minute that Mallory will want you running after him, do you?' he asked nastily. 'He's had what he wanted,' he snarled crudely. 'He won't want you turning up on his doorstep now!'

Phelix felt instantly nauseous again. How did she ever come to have such a father? She could only be glad that she had inherited her mother's traits and not his. But, as it was, she was feeling at her most vulnerable, and wanted to get away from him and his cold house as fast as she could.

'I'm not going to Nathan,' she replied, with what dignity he had left her with.

'So where the devil are you going?' he questioned disagreeably.

'I haven't decided yet.' She hadn't, but she doubted he would want her forwarding address. 'I won't be coming back,' she added finally, and, there being nothing else to say, she went to turn from him.

But, as ever, he wanted the last word. 'It worked, then, didn't it?' he snarled.

She really wasn't interested, but years of giving him the courtesy of hearing what he had to say had become something of a well-mannered habit. 'What worked?' she asked, knowing even as she asked that she would be much better just getting out of there.

'Mallory! He set you up!'

She should have guessed. Her father was not the sort to give in gracefully. 'Why?' she asked. 'To get back at you?' she challenged.

He shook his head. 'He set you up, and you fell for it.'

'I don't need to hear this,' Phelix attempted, turning away again.

'Tell you he loved you, did he?' She turned back, her face burning. 'Of course he did!' Edward Bradbury cried triumphantly. 'And you believed him. You must have been a push-over!'

Nausea gripped her. She did not want to hear this. Did not want her father undermining her confidence the way he had so often tried to—and so often succeeded—in the past.

'Well, you soon saw him off, didn't you?' She refused to be subdued.

'Why wouldn't I? It was only on Friday that he was telling me point-blank how he intended to divorce you at his very first opportunity!'

Her breath caught. She had no idea what the situation between her and Nathan now was, had been too enraptured by him to think past the moment. But she did not care at all for

the thought that he might have been discussing the subject o
their marriage—none or otherwise—with her father. *If* such
discussion had taken place! But—had it?

And Edward Bradbury must have read that hint of doubt i
her face, because, 'Ask him,' he challenged. 'The very next tim
you see him, ask him if he did not say those very words. Unles
he's the biggest liar breathing, he'll admit it.'

Phelix could think of no particular reason why Nathan woul
lie about such a thing. But doubt—about Nathan this time—an
uncertainty she did not want, doubt she had thought she had don
away with, was there to plague her again. If Nathan had told he
father that he wanted to divorce her with all speed, then it mus
have been a lie when Nathan had told her that he loved her!

She felt on very shaky ground suddenly. 'I know Natha
Mallory far better than you're ever likely to,' her fathe
pressed on. 'He's an unforgiving man and will get back at m
any way he can.'

'Can you blame him after what you did to him?' Phelix rallied

'Any way he can,' Edward Bradbury ploughed on, ignorin
what she had just said. 'Even to the extent of using m
daughter to do so.'

No! She did not want to hear this! 'I'm sure you're right,
she agreed calmly. Anything to get out of there.

'You *know* I'm right!' her father insisted. 'But it's gone pas
him getting even with me. It's now more to do with that out
sourcing contract.' Phelix looked at him in some surprise
'Mallory knows damned well that I'm in a better position tha
he is to snaffle that deal,' he went on. 'That contract is as goo
as signed in my favour.'

Phelix stared at him. That didn't make sense. 'I can hardl
believe that.' She dug her heels in. 'Why, if you've got tha
contract virtually done and dusted, are all the big chiefs goin
to Switzerland next week?' she challenged.

'Because certain form has to be observed, naturally. Th

others don't know what I know in any case. That's why Mallory has come sniffing around after you.' Was she really this crude man's daughter? Sometimes she just couldn't believe it. 'Though, given that any man will take what's on offer,' he sneered crudely, 'it's not you he's after—creeping in here behind my back. He knew I wouldn't be here.' He chipped away a bit more of her confidence. 'He knows you work in my legal department—a misplaced word here, a detail of the contract being negotiated falling in the wrong ear, and what do you know? The Mallorys are back in with a chance—a chance of offering a better contract before all signatures are down.'

Phelix had to concede that—although she doubted very much that she would be the main legal executive dealing with any such mammoth contract—some parts of it might well drop on to her desk.

Doubts were already building up and starting to spear her with their spiteful barbs when Edward Bradbury put the final boot in. 'As soon as he knew you'd be in Davos last week, he flew out to charm you witless.'

Phelix stared at her father. 'Nathan had no idea at all that I'd even be *in* Davos last week!' she protested. Of that she *was* certain.

'*Of course* he knew! He planned it right down to the last detail.'

She would not believe it. 'Nathan wasn't even going to Davos last week. But for one of his people being unable to attend—'

'And who do you suppose ordered that person not to attend?'

'I don't believe you.' She wanted to run, but would not. Her father was not going to have the last word this time. 'Nathan only went because—'

'Because he knew you would be there, and he saw a splendid chance. A whole week to have a crack at you! What could be better?'

'You're wrong!'

'You know I'm not. Any one of his underlings would more normally have stepped in to give that speech without one of the high-ups—Mallory himself—putting themselves out to take it on.'

No! But even as she thought no, her intelligence was telling her that it was true. Nathan could have sent any one of his scientist workforce in his stead. There had been absolutely *no reason* for him to go in person. And it would have been far more likely, surely, for him to send someone else?

Suddenly her whole world was starting to fall apart. But what she lacked in confidence, she had in an abundance of pride.

'I don't believe you!' she stated loftily.

'Don't!' Her father was angry. 'Don't believe me! You just go ahead and make a fool of yourself!' He started to rampage. 'But believe this, I know men better than you do. I know men like Mallory, much, much better than you'll ever know him. So don't imagine for a moment that he wants to stay married to you. Because he doesn't. You're good for his purpose, that's all.' He was starting to raise his voice. 'All he's interested in is finding out what we're doing on the outsource deal. With you on-side he'll reckon he's got it made. The bastard's an expert,' he raged on. 'He knew where you would be all last week! It was no coincidence that he stayed in the same hotel.' He did not wait for her to interrupt when her lips parted, but pounded furiously on. 'Every firm of note is charged up to get that outsourcing contact. You were his insurance in the event Bradbury's got it. He set out to woo you,' he spat. 'Bed you if he had to, but above all else get everything he wanted to know from you—and if it might take longer than a week or so to learn snippets of contract talk and special clauses, he was prepared for that—'

'Stop it!' Her father had ranted and raved at her before, but never had it hurt as much as this. 'Stop it,' she mumbled unhappily.

But Edward Bradbury knew that he had planted enough seeds to ensure that Nathan Mallory would get short shrift the next time he approached his daughter.

'Willingly,' he replied. 'Just don't come crying to me when divorce papers land on your desk—any time soon.'

'You can be certain I won't do that!' she answered stiffly, and got out of there before her father should witness her final humiliation—her tears.

She made it to her car without breaking down, and drove to a lay-by, where she sat for an age getting herself together.

Away from the house, away from her father, she was sure she did not believe a word of it. But those words he had spoken had a nasty way of returning again and again to pick at her.

She just did not believe that Nathan had known she would be in Switzerland last week. She drew a shaky catch of a breath as logic she did not want reasoned that, with the trip being planned quite some weeks ago, if, as he father had said, Nathan had deliberately 'targeted' her, then he could quite easily have found out that information.

Not that he could have known in advance which hotel she was staying in. She brightened up. Henry had switched her hotel at the last minute. So the fact that Nathan was staying in the same hotel must be, as she had thought, pure coincidence and nothing more.

Phelix brightened some more to be able to put her father's diabolical suspicions from her. In any event, prior to Switzerland, the last time Nathan had seen her she had been plain, immature and clueless. He had been kind to her eight years ago, she recalled, but they had not seen each other since then. He had not seen her, so she just could not see him deliberately setting out to 'woo', as her father had put it, the type of female she had been then, regardless of that contract.

Her brightness faded when thoughts she did not want rushed in to remind her of the many, many millions that contract would be worth over the next ten years. It faded further when she recalled how Henry and Nathan seemed to bump into each other every so often. Nathan had known she was a career woman. What else had Henry told him? That she had shed her dowdy image and had scrubbed up rather well? That, surely would have made the pill easier to swallow?

Suddenly Phelix was back to doubting again. Oh, Nathan she mourned. It was all so different when she was with him But those doubts, those doubts that had rocketed in when apart from him in Switzerland, were there swamping her again.

Feeling quite desperate, she made herself remember those times when she had been with him. Those times when he would make her laugh. She had loved laughing with him. Loved him

She remembered being in his arms last night. Surely no man could be so tender and feel nothing? She had thrilled to his kisses, his touch, his lovemaking…

But her father and his 'he'd bed you if he had to' began to sully that beautiful memory. Surely Nathan had not purposely set about seducing her? Even to the extent of telling her he loved her? She could not believe that. And yet—what did she know of men? Apart from having had little time for much of a social life, what with work and study, she had just never been able to let any man get close to her—before Nathan…

But why would he tell her father he was going to divorce her at his first opportunity? If Nathan *had* said that, of course.

Well, it was for certain she could not ask him. To do so might give him the impression that she was trying to hang on to him—and her pride would not allow that.

Had he said it? Did it matter anyway? They may have made love with each other but that did not signify any sort of commitment on his part. Phelix was feeling so thoroughly mixed up by then that she had no idea what it meant on her part either—other than that she wanted with all her being that he had taken her with love in his heart for her.

By the time she drove away from the lay-by she was starting to feel more confused than ever. She booked into the first respectable-looking hotel she came to, and was by then reduced to feeling totally numb.

She lay on her hotel bed, her head starting to ache from the punishment of her whirling brain. She did not believe it. Did not, would not believe that Nathan had deliberately set her up to get her on his side with regard to any information she could feed him.

And yet—had Nathan set out to make her fall in love with him? Did he *know* that she was in love with him? He must do. He had the evidence that she did not give herself to just any man—which made him special. Oh, she couldn't bear it!

Phelix was again trying to dissect. Had Nathan known she was Switzerland-bound before she had gone there, before *he* had gone there? If so, it would mean that her father was right, that— The ringing of her mobile phone cut into her thoughts.

Very few people had her cellphone number, and she certainly did not want to speak to her father. Though she rather thought he had said more than enough without thinking to phone her to add more.

But it might just be Henry. Perhaps she could ask him… She reached for her mobile. 'Hello?' she said, and nearly dropped it.

'Phelix, are you all right?' Nathan asked.

Tears sprang to her eyes. She swallowed them down. 'How did you get hold of this number?' she asked with what wit she could find.

'With difficulty. I've been ringing Henry—he was out. Are you all right, my darling?' he asked. That 'my darling' threatened to sink her. 'I regretted leaving you with that monster before I'd gone a mile.'

'I'm fine,' she told him flatly.

'I've been ringing your landline—only to get an earful from your father. But we can deal with him later. I'm outside your house now. Say the word and I'll come in and get you.'

Oh, Nathan. 'Er—I'm not at home,' she answered. 'I've—moved out.'

'You have! Good! That was my next suggestion.' She could

tell he was smiling. Just that and her backbone was evaporating. It would not do. 'Tell me where you are and I'll—'

'Nathan.' She just had to cut in. That, or go along with whatever Nathan said, regardless of whether he was just stringing her along or not. She knew that she could not ask him if he had told her father that he intended to divorce her because that would cause him to presuppose that she had thought she would stay married to him. But there was one question that she *could* ask him. 'Did you know I would be in Davos before you decided to go to Switzerland yourself?' she asked him.

And rather thought she had her answer in the slight pause that followed, before, 'You sound serious?' Nathan answered quietly.

Was he playing for time? 'Did you?' she persisted—and could have wept at his answer.

'Yes, I knew,' he admitted. 'What has—'

'Was I—?' She broke off, feeling foolish even before she voiced the question. 'Was I, in any way, any part of your reason for deciding to personally attend?' She made herself continue.

And again there was a pause. 'I confess, little love, you were very much a part of the reason I decided to attend,' he replied.

Gripping tightly on to her telephone, Phelix sank down onto the bed. 'Thank you, Nathan,' she said, thanking him for at least being honest in that. But pride was rearing and pushing her to not allow him to think that she was clinging to him because of what had happened between them. 'I don't think we have anything more to say to each other,' she told him coolly. 'Goodbye,' she added, finality in her tone. She did not wait for him to answer but abruptly cut the call. He, Nathan, her love, *had set her up!*

If Nathan rang again—which she thought extremely unlikely after the way she had just spoken to him—Phelix was unaware of it. She immediately switched her phone off and had not the smallest interest in checking to see if there were any messages.

That Sunday that had started out so blissfully ended as one of the worst Sundays of her life.

She lay awake for hours that night, going over every moment she had spent with Nathan. And every moment seemed to bear out what her father had said about Nathan setting her up to get her on-side.

He had been there from the first, she remembered, coming over to her the moment she had appeared at the conference centre. But not by word or look had he revealed that he had known she would be there.

He had, that very same day, 'bumped into her' in the park. Had asked her to dine with him that night, she recalled. Had the very next day followed her to the funicular.

She had dined with him that same night—and he had been there at the swimming pool the very next morning—and then they had walked up the mountain together.

All in all, she realised, they had seemed to spend a considerable amount of time with each other. And all, as far as he was concerned, in the interests of big business!

After a fitful night's sleep, Phelix awoke and knew that she had had it with big business. She was in no hurry to go to her office. In fact, were it not for Henry, she would not have gone at all. But, at a little before three that afternoon, she sat in her office and typed out a letter, and then went to see Henry.

Luckily he was alone, and welcomed her with a smile the way he always did. Though as she approached his desk his smile changed to a look of disquiet.

'You look troubled?' he questioned straight away.

'My resignation,' she replied, and handed him the letter she had just signed.

'Take a seat, Phelix,' he invited, 'and talk to me.'

She took a shaky breath. Where to start? How much to tell? 'I had a bit of an upset—well, a lot of an upset with my father yesterday.'

'He's home?'

'Unexpectedly,' she answered with a shaky sigh. 'I was with Nathan Mallory.'

'Out—or at home?'

'At home.'

'That wouldn't have gone down well.'

'It didn't. He none too politely told Nathan to leave. Which he did.'

Henry looked into her eyes, sad eyes, as she relived that awful scene. 'And when he'd gone your father directed his spleen on you?'

'You know what he's like!' Phelix swallowed on a lump in her throat, and went on, 'Grace walked out last week and won't be coming back—I couldn't see any point in staying either.'

'You've left home!' Henry exclaimed, and, not needing an answer, 'Where are you staying?' he asked, and offered, 'You can put up at my place if…'

'That's kind of you, Henry, but I'm comfortable where I am for the moment. I'll start looking round for somewhere to rent or buy tomorrow.'

Henry did not press her, but stated, 'Nathan Mallory was trying to get in touch with you yesterday.'

'He rang my mobile.'

'I didn't think you'd object to my giving him your number,' Henry commented, adding, 'Naturally I wouldn't have given it to him if I didn't know him to be a man of the highest integrity.'

That startled her. Henry, nobody's fool, was usually a fine judge of character. 'You—think he has high integrity?' she questioned slowly.

'Of course,' Henry answered without hesitation. 'I wouldn't have recommended him to Oscar Livingstone had I not heard and received extremely good reports of him. Nothing he has done since has done anything to change my good opinion of him.'

Phelix stared at Henry, her insides starting to knot up. 'You've—er—heard good reports of him?'

'Bearing in mind that seldom a week goes by without I bump into one industrialist or another, had there been anything in any way detrimental being said of Nathan Mallory or his company you can be sure I'd have heard about it,' Henry replied.

And all at once Phelix was suddenly feeling totally mixed up again. But she fought her way through the quagmire that was in her head. 'Would you say, from what you know and have heard of him, that Nathan was capable of pulling any trick in the book to get this JEPC Holdings outsourcing contract?'

Henry looked at her, but, when there must have been questions queuing up in his mind, he instead stayed with the point and answered the question she had asked him.

'I don't doubt that Nathan Mallory can be as hard-headed as the next man when it comes to business—he would have to be to have made such a success of the company after that near financial crash eight years ago, when a lot of companies went to the wall. He's shrewd, Phelix, I'll grant that, but from what I've witnessed of him I would say that to act unfairly is beneath him. I'm afraid that when it comes to dirty tricks it's your father who wears that crown.'

Her breath caught, and she desperately needed to be by herself. But she had just one last question. 'Would you say that he—Nathan—is a man to be trusted?' she asked.

And Henry, without having to think about it, nodded. 'I would say that he is entirely trustworthy,' he confirmed.

Phelix stood up. 'I'll—er—go and clear out my desk,' she said, and urgently needed solitude.

'I'm on my way out,' Henry said, having shown no signs of being in a hurry but appearing to have had all day to talk to her if it would take the troubled look from her face. 'I'll give you a ring at the end of the week. We could catch up over a meal,' he suggested.

'I'd like that,' she agreed, and made it back to her own office to close the door and to sink in her chair, her head in turmoil.

Had she been wrong?

That question haunted and occupied her for the next hour as she sought to untangle fact from emotion, lie and deceit from truth.

And at the end of that hour, with her cheeks pink from the stress of it, a picture had emerged of her—despite her best efforts to the contrary—having still been so much under the insidious and devious influence of her father that she had needed to hear Henry speak highly of Nathan for her to start to see everything from an opposite perspective.

And that left her having to ask: had she not only been wrong, but, in acting the way she had in believing her father, had she wronged Nathan?

With her mouth dry, Phelix went over everything again, starting with Nathan knowing in advance that she would be in Davos. He had come straight over, had not pretended not to know her, but had said straight out 'How are you, Phelix?'

He had not revealed, in stating that they knew each other from way back, that they had actually married each other. But given that that did not make it any clearer to know why he had made that trip when he had known she would be there, what was more natural than that he would want to have some sort of private discussion with her?

Which was why he had 'bumped into her' in that park that same afternoon. And, having deduced from what she had said that Henry could well have been the one to have put him in touch with Oscar Livingstone, what was more natural, too, than that he would follow her to that funicular so as to have more private conversation?

Not that they had spoken very much about Henry then, she recalled. That had come later. But had that—the two of them being together a lot of the time—all been the act of a man out to get her on-side with regard to what he might glean in respect of that wretched contract? Or, and a very breath-taking or, were all of Nathan's following actions those of a man—starting to—fall in love!

Phelix went hot all over. Oh, my heavens! She tried not to get too excited—it was difficult. She loved him. She knew that she did. But could he—love her? She swallowed hard—and suddenly came alive.

What a fool she had been! Good heavens, hadn't she thought, that night her control freak father had telephoned her at her hotel when she had told him she had dined with Nathan, that her father would spoil it for her if he could?

And he darn near had! Might well still have done. Would Nathan ever want to speak to her again? She doubted that anyone had ever terminated a telephone conversation with him so abruptly, or so finally either. She, with her cool, 'I don't think we have anything more to say to each other.' Oh, heavens, how *could* she?

Phelix remembered that day they had walked down the mountain, and how Nathan would have taken her to lunch with the business people he was meeting. He had trusted her. *Had trusted her!* And—even after he had said that he loved her—her trust in him had not endured beyond that one wonderful night.

Phelix stopped hurting and started to fully trust the man she loved. She started to hope.

But she was the one in the wrong here. And if Nathan would ever speak to her again, it was up to her to put it right. Or at least to try. Nathan had his pride too—he would not be the one to contact her.

She recalled his mammoth pride when, facing ruin, he had refused to touch a penny of the Bradbury money—and she realised she would be fortunate if he did not tell her to go take a running jump.

Phelix looked at the phone on her desk. 'Learn to trust your instincts,' he had once told her. And it seemed to her then that, were she brave enough, there was only one thing that she could do.

She did not have his home number. But he could well be at his office, and she did know the name of his company. She looked it up in the telephone directory and, feeling on very shaky ground, took a deep breath—and dialled.

For the last time, though the ink was now dry on her resignation, she used what clout there was to be had in telling the receptionist, 'Phelix Bradbury of Edward Bradbury Systems. Mr Nathan Mallory, please.'

It worked in that in no time she was put through to his PA. But that was where, her insides so much of a mish-mash, disappointment awaited her.

'Mr Mallory is not in the building,' the PA informed her pleasantly. 'Can I help at all? He's not expected back.'

'That's very kind of you. But I need to speak with Nathan personally,' Phelix replied, having braved herself to make the call, not knowing if she was glad or sorry that he wasn't in. 'I'll try him in the morning,' she attempted, hoping to find the same courage by then that she had found so far.

'If you'd like to leave a message?' the PA offered, adding, 'It's unlikely that he'll be available for the rest of this week.'

Bells rang, and Phelix realised she had been so caught up with matters personal that she had forgotten that anybody who was anybody in the scientific engineering world would be out of the country from tomorrow on.

'Switzerland,' she said without thinking.

'You know about it, of course.'

'I was there myself last week,' Phelix found she was volunteering. But, getting herself a little more together, 'Not to worry. I'll... It's not important,' she lied. Not important! It was just about the most important communication of her life!

Phelix left the Bradbury building, guessing that Nathan had either left his office to fly to Zurich or had gone home early prior to flying out—most likely with his father—the following morning. They would want to be there in good time for the round of talks that were to begin on Wednesday.

She returned to her hotel, but only to spend the next few hours with her thoughts constantly on Nathan and with such a yearning to see him in her heart that she did not know how to bear it.

She went to bed early and lay awake, sleepless, only to get up early on Tuesday with that ache for Nathan rising with her. She wondered when he would be coming home—and would she have the nerve to again ring his office?

In an attempt to fix her thoughts on something else, she left her hotel and headed for the estate agents. But with no idea what sort of accommodation she was looking for she just stood looking at the properties photographed in the estate agent's window—and was suddenly frustrated with the whole idea. She didn't know what she wanted…

Yes, she did! She wanted Nathan. She caught sight of her reflection in the window. Saw a dark-haired slender woman there—a woman Nathan had once called beautiful, a woman he had once said 'I love you' to—and all at once she knew she could not wait. And in that moment her mind was made up.

She could not go on like this. Not while there was a chance. Nathan trusted her; she would trust him. Her heart began to hammer. He had said he loved her. Loved *her*!

She would go to him. 'You must never do anything that doesn't feel one hundred percent right to you,' he had once said to her. But to go to him did seem right.

Phelix was on a plane winging its way to Zurich that afternoon when she started to wonder if she *was* doing the right thing. Pride and fear that Nathan might tell her *You must be joking* when she turned up at his hotel, attempted to steer her away from journeying on to Davos.

She pushed fear of rejection from her and made herself remember that he had told her he loved her. But—was she being very naïve? She did not want his telling her he loved her to be just a thing of the moment. Something meaningless that men said when in the throes of lovemaking.

Then she remembered Nathan's tender lovemaking, the way he had cradled her to him afterwards, gently stroking her hair, making sure everything was all right with her. He had called her 'sweet darling' afterwards, and gently kissed her, and held her as if he never wanted to let her go.

Her world had righted itself by the time Phelix had collected a car and had pointed it in the direction of Davos Platz.

But when, some hours later, she pulled up in the hotel car park, she was a total mass of nerves and was most reluctant to get out of the car.

She did not even know that Nathan was staying at this hotel, for goodness' sake! He could well have cancelled his booking and moved on elsewhere. And even if he was staying here he could well be out with his father somewhere, having dinner.

Oh, dear heaven, she felt close to tears. What if Nathan refused to see her? Refused to speak to her? She could hardly blame him—not after the way she had been to him on the phone.

Suddenly then Phelix had a moment of courage and, not wanting to be hampered with her luggage, she left the car and went as quickly as she could into the hotel.

Having thought until she could think no more, she took the lift up to the fifth floor, knowing that Nathan would know, since there was no good business reason why she was there, that she had journeyed to Switzerland solely to see him.

With nerves biting she knocked on the door that had used to be his and waited. She heard a sound inside and wanted to disappear. But, when she had never run after a man in her life, and would have said the chances of her doing so were ridiculous, she found she could not run away. She was paralysed.

Then the door opened, and as scarlet colour flooded her face she swallowed on a severely dry throat. The room had not been appointed to someone else. Tall, dark-haired, and with a wonderful mouth, Nathan stood there.

He stared at her with grey eyes that for a brief mistaken moment she thought lit up to see her. But in the next brief moment, as he coolly looked back at her, she had to accept that that was just so much wishful thinking on her part.

Though he did seem as speechless as her. But not for long. And when he did speak it was not, as she had feared, to tell her to get lost, but to state in a short, cold tone, his eyes steady on her nervous expression, 'You took your time!' But when she was starting to fear he might yet slam the door hard shut in her face, he opened it wider. 'You'd better come in,' he invited, but did not sound too welcoming!

CHAPTER NINE

PHELIX preceded Nathan along the short hall. The room was similar to the one she had used. A double bed tucked away in a large curtained-off alcove with a sitting room in front of it. She heard the door close quietly behind her and her mouth went dry.

Nathan had been expecting her? 'You took your time,' he had said. Had he been expecting her to make the journey from England to Switzerland?

She made it to the centre of the room, and turned around. Oh, how dear he was to her! 'You—knew I was on my way here?' she questioned, her voice husky with nerves. Except for telling her hotel in London that she was going away for a few days, she had notified no one else.

Nathan solemnly studied her. She hoped her colour had died down. 'I rang my PA after lunch. She told me you'd phoned yesterday—but that it wasn't important,' he informed her. He looked at her expectantly, but she couldn't speak. She had come all this way, and suddenly she had lost her voice. But Nathan was still looking at her intently. 'Was it important after all?' he asked. But still the words would not come. And Nathan, still waiting, watching and waiting, taking in the shadows beneath her eyes, leaned back against the wall, and went on thoughtfully, 'It seems to me, and I could well be mistaken here, that for you to have picked up your passport and come here to see me would make it very important to you, in some way.'

Phelix opened her mouth, but the words she wanted to say just would not come, no matter how much she urged them. And instead she found she was blurting out, 'I've resigned my job—with immediate effect.'

Nathan did not look too impressed. 'You're saying that since you had nothing better to do you thought you'd take a flight—?'

'No!' she protested. And, as realisation struck, 'You're not going to make this easy for me, are you?' He did not answer, and Phelix swallowed on a dry throat. Be brave, she instructed, but was not feeling very brave. Though she did find her voice to admit, 'You—are not mistaken. This—to see you—is important to me.'

Whether Nathan could see that she was under some kind of stress—all her life she had kept her feelings battened down—she did not know but, even though his tone was still cool, he unbent sufficiently to suggest, 'Why not take a seat and tell me about it?'

She was glad of the offer. She went and took a seat on the sofa, Nathan took the chair to the side of it. 'I—er…' she began, and could have wept that the words she needed seemed to be locked up in her throat.

But as she struggled, so Nathan seemed to relent a little. 'Tell me,' he prompted.

'I…' She tried, and then suddenly she felt stronger. 'I—wronged you. I—um—wanted to apologise.'

He stared at her, his expression unsmiling. 'That's a fair trip to say sorry,' he commented.

She looked at him. He looked tired—as if he, like her, had spent a few sleepless nights. 'I've—had a few—er—trust issues,' she confessed.

Nathan nodded. 'Let me guess—your father put the boot in where I was concerned, and did it so successfully you didn't know where the hell you were?'

'That about sums it up,' she admitted.

'You know where you are now?'

She wished that he would hold her. Phelix felt she would be much better able to talk to him about things that were personal to her and to him if Nathan would just hold her. One arm around her shoulders would be enough. But, no, she had hurt him, and his pride, by refusing to trust him and, as she had thought, he was not going to make it easy for her.

Or... As she looked at him, something seemed to click. By telling her that he loved her, Nathan, much more sensitive than she had realised, had laid himself bare. She had, so to speak, thrown that love back at him, rendering *him*—vulnerable. And he, all male, did not like it.

But his expression was solemn still, giving no hint that he might care so much as a button for her. 'Yes, I know where I am now,' she agreed quietly, and, because she felt he needed to know, 'For years I have been put down by my father. He has attempted and very often succeeded in undermining my confidence.'

'With all you have going for you—your brain and your beauty—you are still short on confidence?'

Oh, Nathan—he thought she had beauty. Her heart melted. She was all his—couldn't he see that? But a dreadful thought suddenly struck her that perhaps, after the way she had seemingly rejected his love, she had killed any feelings he had for her!

But she didn't want to think like that. Would not think like that. She would trust. That was why she was here—because she trusted Nathan.

'My father is very clever; he can be subtle when he needs to be. But, sharp or mean, he never lets up chipping away at me.' She hated talking about her father this way. But Nathan was far more important to her than any totally undeserved loyalty to her father. 'I thought I had grown away from his power to get to me. And I was sure I had. Only—' Phelix broke off, the words to tell Nathan of her feelings for him wedged tightly in her throat.

'Only?' he prompted.

'Only…' she tried, and forged quickly ahead. 'Only I'd never—er—um—cared about any m-man the way I had feelings for… And—and, well, I expect, think, I must have left myself rather exposed.'

Phelix dared a look at Nathan then. She knew her colour was high, knew that he had observed it. But his expression did not change, was stern, if anything, when, as if intent on making her push through the barriers built up in her over the years of living with her unfeeling father, he asked, 'Am I to suppose, Phelix, that I am the man you care about?'

And that annoyed her. 'You can *ask*?' she challenged warmly. 'After what we…'

'There are more ways of saying you care for someone than by making love with them,' he replied bluntly.

And that was it as far as she was concerned. She got up from the sofa, and, as he stood up too, 'You're not going to forgive me, are you?' she asked, not needing an answer. 'There's nothing more to be said,' she stated proudly—and would have walked by him, heading for the door. But before she had gone two steps she felt Nathan's hand, firm on her arm, halting her, turning her round to face him.

'Oh, no,' he said shortly. 'You may be academically bright, but emotionally you're all at sea. But you've put me through hell, Phelix Bradbury, and you're not getting away with it that easily.'

She pulled to try and shake his hand from her arm. It did no good, but only made matters worse in that Nathan's other hand came up to her other arm to hold her still. But she was angry with him still—how much more of her pride did he expect her to ditch, for goodness' sake?

'You think you're the only one who's had sleepless nights?' she charged shortly. Love him to bits though she might, there *were* limits. Besides, what confidence she had found was already starting to crumble.

'Serves you right!' he answered toughly. But then, as he looked at her, suddenly his tone was changing. 'Oh, hell,' he groaned. 'I can't stay mad at you!' And it was less harshly that he said, 'We've come a long way these last eight days, Phelix. I've watched you blossom from a proud but cool woman, with a permanent touch-me-not air, to a warm, wonderful and responsive woman. I've watched and admired as you have pushed your way through your bottled up emotions, and I've—waited.'

'Waited?' she queried, needing her wits about her. But his hold on her, just his touch, was making a nonsense of her attempt at logical thinking.

Nathan looked deeply into her wide green eyes. 'You know how things are with me,' he said steadily. 'You've intimated you care for me. Have—?'

'Are th-things still the same with you?' she asked, suddenly feeling so nervous she didn't know if he realised that she was asking him if he still loved her.

He shook his head. And she nearly died in fear that she, by her lack of trust, had forfeited his love. But it was not that. 'You know,' he said, just that short sentence, and she realised then that, having declared he loved her, he was not going to repeat it while she was still holding back.

'I—trust you,' she responded.

'You're sure?'

She would have thought that the fact she was her in Davos with him proved that—but only then did she see the extent of the hurt she had caused him.

'I'm so sorry,' she apologised again, and, needing a clear head suddenly, made to move away from him. When he saw that she was making for the sofa, and not the door, he let her go. She re-took her seat and waited until he had resumed his seat in the chair he had vacated, then, trying to put events into some kind of sequence order, she began to explain. 'I was still in some kind of w-wonderland when my father charged into my bedroom on—er…'

'Sunday morning,' Nathan put in quietly.

She tried to smile her thanks but, remembering the horror of it, her smile did not quite make it. 'I've had years of my father shouting and bellowing about the place, but all that happening in my bedroom after—' She broke off to take a shaky breath. 'Anyway, my emotions were all churned up without me suddenly realising there was a thunderstorm going on. There were you, having eight years previously been done down by my father, now being screeched at by him for your trouble. There was him, his face contorted the way it was that night…that night…' She was choked suddenly.

But, as if all at once seeing that there was more trauma in her life than he had known about, as if her suddenly haunted expression was more than he could take, Nathan had quickly left his chair and was sitting next to her, his hands holding hers.

'That night?' he pressed quietly.

And she did trust him, and for the first time ever something unlocked in her and she found she was able to confide in this man she trusted. 'That night, the night my mother died, there was a terrible storm.' She paused, but, as if sensing that she needed to get this said and out of her system, out into the open, Nathan did not interrupt her. 'My parents had separate rooms—the thunder woke me,' she went on, her voice staccato. 'My mother didn't like storms either, so I went along to her room to check that she was all right.' Phelix took another shaky breath. 'She was not all right.' She relived the awful scene. 'Apart from the flashes of lightning, the room was in darkness. But my father was there. In the lightning his face was evil, enraged and evil…' Her voice petered out. Nathan's grip on her hands firmed, and she gained strength to whisper, 'He was assaulting her.'

'Oh, my darling!' All pretence at being aloof fell from Nathan as he gathered Phelix in his arms and held her.

'My mother was a gentle genteel person. She left home that night.' Phelix wanted it all said now. 'That is, my mother had always planned to leave my father, but he said she would have to leave me behind, and she couldn't face leaving me to be brought up alone and by him. But that night she couldn't take any more. I've since learned that she phoned Henry—he told me last Friday that he had always hoped to marry her—though my mother never knew. They were just very good friends then. She needed one, a friend. Anyhow, she could not take any more abuse after that, and rang Henry. She was out in the road when she was struck by a car.'

Tenderly Nathan kissed her brow. 'Go on,' he urged gently.

'That's about it, really, other than each time there's a violent thunderstorm I still see that scene, the evil in my father's face, my mother pleading with him.' She took a shaky breath, and, having released that awful memory for the first time, began again, 'So there we were last Sunday morning—strangely I wasn't aware of the storm going on until my father came in raging—and shame such as I'd never experienced swamped me.'

'Not shame because of what had taken place between us?'

'No!' she exclaimed. 'I was totally enchanted by what had happened,' she confessed, without meaning to. Nathan's arms about her tightened, and she hurried on, wanting all the stomach-churning sickness of it said and finished with. 'I was embarrassed—mortified—for you! There you were on the receiving end of my father's rancour, there was my father spitting vitriol, and there was lightning and thunder crashing about reminding me of that other ghastly scene.'

'Sweet love,' Nathan murmured. And, having got everything out into the open, having wanted everything said and done, it seemed as if Nathan understood that she needed to be free of it all, understood that she needed to get this out of her system, because, 'Finish it, Phelix,' he bade her gently.

'There's not much more. I was being crucified on Sunday

›y thoughts of how awful it must be for you to be embroiled n such an ugly scene. I was drowning in the humiliation of ›eing certain that, while it was not such a rare experience for ne, such scenes had never taken place in your family home. I ust wanted you to go. Did not want that you should be dragged nto it, have to suffer and be part of it.'

'I wanted to take you with me,' Nathan owned.

'Did you?' Phelix asked, believing him, feeling choked.

'More than anything,' he admitted. 'But against that you vere telling me to go. And while I was able to ignore your 'ather, I could not ignore you, or the fact that from the way 'ou were gripping on to that bedsheet—apart from my knowl-:dge of your modesty—I knew there was no way you were ;oing to get out of that bed with both me and your father tanding there.'

Phelix went a shade pink. She had been naked apart from hat sheet, and Nathan had known that. He must have recalled oo how the night before she had needed the light out before he had been able to shed her clothes in front of him.

'You're probably right,' she had to agree. 'Though I wanted 'ou to ask me to go with you.'

Gently Nathan placed his lips on hers. 'Dear Phelix,' he ›reathed. 'I came back for you when your father kept blocking ny phone calls. I wasn't sure if I'd be making matters better ›r worse if I came up to the house, so stayed outside…'

'And then got my mobile number from Henry?'

'After a long wait.'

'I wasn't very nice to you—I'm sorry,' she apologised.

'I could have throttled you,' Nathan stated, but there was a varmth for her there in his eyes as he said it. 'I knew after that all that your father had got to you. I'd no idea what he told 'ou, but how could you believe him—after what we had hared? I thought I had your trust. I—'

'I'm sorry,' Phelix burst in to apologise again. 'I really am.

It's just that I have a bit of—um—difficulty getting close to someone, and—er…'

'And—er…?' Nathan prompted.

'I'm—learning.'

'I'll teach you,' he promised, with such a wonderful smile she just had to smile back.

'I went to see Henry—to hand in my resignation,' she added. 'I'd been in a bit of a stew,' she confessed. 'My father had done his work well. But then there was Henry, telling me more or less how he would trust you above my father—and I began to see everything from a different angle.

'You started to really trust that when I told you I loved you, I meant it?'

'Oh, Nathan!' she whispered, tears springing to her eyes.

'Don't you dare cry on me!' he instructed swiftly.

And she laughed. Oh, how she loved him. 'Are you going to forgive me?' she asked.

'For so cold-heartedly telling me goodbye after I'd declared my heart is yours?'

'I made you angry?'

'Livid,' he answered cheerfully. 'And I'll admit all over the place emotionally. I flew here yesterday to stop myself coming to look for you.'

'You would have tried to find me?'

'As I saw it, I had two options. Either I came looking for you—when from the way you'd ended my call you would probably slam the door in my face for my trouble. Or I could leave you to work things out in your own time and then, hopefully, if you loved me even half as much as I loved you, *you* would come looking for me.'

Phelix had to smile again, her heart full to bursting. She hadn't been able to tell Nathan that she loved him, but he knew. Apart from so willingly giving herself to him, the very fact that she was here in Switzerland—having come looking for him—told him that she loved him.

'I rang your PA…'

'That's when I started to hope I wouldn't have to come looking for you.'

'That I'd come to you?'

'I hoped you might ring my PA again. I instructed her in the event that you did to make sure she gave you my mobile number and my home number,' he revealed. 'I hadn't dared to hope you'd hop on a plane to come looking for me. But—here you are,' he said gladly, and pulled her up close and kissed her long and lingeringly, giving her a rueful look and putting some minute space between them. 'As tempting as you are, my lovely darling, I want every doubt you're ever had about me cleared away before—'

'I don't have any doubts,' Phelix answered, knowing now whom she should trust—and who she shouldn't.

'So what did Bradbury say to turn you against me?'

'He could never turn me against you,' she confessed shyly. 'It's just—it's all so new to me, I suppose. When I'm with you everything seems so right. It's just—when you're not there…'

Nathan gave her a loving smile. 'He took advantage of me not being there to defend myself to get to you.'

'He's good at it,' she owned, and, as she felt herself growing in confidence that Nathan did truly love her, she did not want any secrets from him. 'I'm afraid he started to first spoil my memories by saying how you'd set me up. And then, when I wouldn't believe that, he went on to say how you'd used me to get me on-side regarding this wretched JEPC Holdings contact…' She halted when Nathan stared at her in disbelief.

'The man's in a world of his own,' he commented. 'Beyond it being massive, nobody knows for sure exactly what the proposal is yet. And?' he pressed.

'And how you had deliberately targeted me.' Nathan looked interested. 'You don't want to hear the rest of it.' She shied away from telling him what her father had said about Nathan wanting to divorce her. It was a subject she did not want to bring up. She did not care what happened with her and Nathan in the future. It was enough to know that he loved her now.

'And?' Nathan pressed again, determined, it seemed, to have nothing hidden away in dark corners.

'And,' she went bravely on, 'how the only reason you'd come to that conference anyway was because you knew that I would be there. That you could—'

'It's the truth,' Nathan cut in. 'The *only* reason I came was because of you,' he said succinctly.

Her eyes went wide. He had said on the phone that she was very much part of the reason he had decided to attend. But, that speech he'd had to make aside, the *only* reason? For ageless moments she stared at him, but seconds later she had rallied. 'I trust you, Nathan,' she said.

He just had to kiss her. But pulled back to murmur ruefully, 'Let me continue before you cause me to forget everything. 'Over the years—slowly at first as he got to know me—Henry Scott has been feeding me various snippets about the woman I had married. How you were taking this exam or that exam, what a brilliant mind you had, how you were growing daily more and more beautiful. It was Henry, having told me you had an inner beauty as well as an outer beauty, who told me you'd be in Davos last week. By that time I was beginning to wonder if maybe I shouldn't perhaps arrange to see this star of the legal profession myself.'

'Henry…!'

'I've an idea he approves of me.' Nathan smiled. 'Anyhow, when my man had to pull out last week, although I'd already got a substitute lined up, I found myself hesitating.'

'I'm glad you came.'

'So am I!' Nathan answered warmly. 'I was aware of you from the moment you walked in. I knew Ross Dawson, of course, and I was acquainted with Duncan Ward and Chris Watson—the Bradbury team—but surely the absolutely stunning creature standing with them wasn't that bony little scrap Phelix Bradbury!'

'You wouldn't have recognised me if I hadn't been with them?'

'I knew as soon as I looked into your wonderfully gorgeous green eyes that it was you.'

'Oh, Nathan.'

'Dearest Phelix—I was instantly bewitched by you.'

'No?' She couldn't believe it, but recalled, 'We met in the park—that afternoon.'

'I was starting to discover what was to become a vital need to be anywhere where you were.'

Her eyes grew saucer-wide. 'Honestly?' But, thinking of how they had frequently seemed to 'bump' into each other, she did not doubt him. 'Oh, Nathan,' she whispered again.

His mouth curved in the most wonderful smile. 'You were getting to me, my darling,' he said, laying a tender kiss on her mouth. 'Though I rather think you must have touched my heart-strings eight years ago when, while my every instinct was telling me to slam out of your home, I discovered that I just could not abandon you to your terror in that storm.'

Phelix looked at him and came close to telling him that she loved him. But something seemed to be holding her back. So—she kissed him.

'You're coming along very nicely,' Nathan said softly, appreciative of her initiative in kissing him. 'So there am I, my lovely darling, trying to deny what is happening to me…'

'You wanted to deny it?'

'It was turning me into someone I did not recognise,' Nathan replied. 'I was sure it was nothing to me that you were out dining with Dawson.'

'You barely acknowledged me,' Phelix recalled.

'Why would I? It was bad enough that you were with him, without you laughing with him and obviously enjoying his company.'

'You were—jealous?' she asked, astonished.

'You could say that,' he admitted.

'But—but we'd only met again that day!'

'That's what I told myself. What did I care?'

Phelix smiled this time. 'But—you did?'

'Enough to change my mind about returning to London as soon as I'd delivered that speech. Which, incidentally, you nearly messed up for me.'

Oh, she loved him so—loved this closeness, this freedom with each other. 'How?' she had to ask.

'As I was speaking I looked for you, found you—your eyes met mine and my heart started to pound, and for a moment there didn't seem to be anyone else in that room except you and me. And for that split second I forgot every word of what I was talking about.'

'Ooh!' she sighed, and felt able to confide, 'I was going to leave too. As soon as I knew you were there at the conference I was going to catch the next plane.'

'I'm glad you stayed,' Nathan murmured. 'But not so glad last Friday when your father gleefully told me you'd gone home.'

'It was because of Henry.'

'I know that now, but back then, while I'd done my best to tread carefully with you, I was starting to panic that I had frightened you off the night before…'

'When you kissed me,' she supplied, and just had to kiss him again. 'Just in case you have any lingering doubts,' she explained, 'you didn't frighten me off.'

Nathan held her, and kissed her, not in the smallest hurry. But he again pulled firmly away. 'Life was dull, dull, dull without you,' he stated. 'How could you have left without a word?'

'I'm sorry,' she offered.

'I understand—now,' he said, but went on to reveal, 'Though at the time it hurt that you'd left without a word. I was in love and vulnerable,' he explained. 'We had seemed to be getting on so well, but had I read it wrong? Was it *not* just shyness that you hadn't left me a message? Was it that you just didn't care?'

'I didn't know,' she said huskily.

'Didn't know what you were doing to me?' He smiled then. 'So I followed you back to London, but was certain I wasn't going to contact you.'

'You soon made a date with someone else.'

'Oh, I do hope that's a bit of green-eye I hear in your voice,' Nathan offered delightedly.

Phelix looked at him, her heart full. 'True,' she admitted, unable to lie to him.

'With you on my mind the whole time, it wasn't much of a date.' He immediately salved her feelings. 'I was driving near your home when the storm that had been threatening suddenly erupted.'

'You remembered my fear of storms?'

Nathan nodded. 'And that if you were home you'd be in that mausoleum of a house all on your own.'

'I was so pleased to see you,' she admitted. 'And—' shyly '—that you stayed.'

Tenderly they kissed. And, as if they could no longer resist each other, they kissed and held, and kissed again.

'Trust me now?' he asked.

'Oh, I do,' she replied. 'When I think of how you have trusted me, I can't bear to think of how I doubted you.'

'You're forgiven,' Nathan said warmly.

'You'd have taken me with you to your business lunch that day. Do you remember—the day we walked down the mountain?'

'I would have,' he replied without hesitation. 'It was a defining moment.'

'Defining?'

'I knew then that I was sunk,' he confessed cheerfully. 'To have included you in that business meal would have been against everything I know. Yet I didn't want to part from you. I just wanted to be near you,' he said simply, and went on,

'Which is why I was so impossible when, looking forward to dinner with you on Thursday, you had the nerve to tell me you couldn't make it.'

'It was either that or have my father join us.'

'A fate worse than death.' Nathan grinned, and kissed her, and confessed, 'I was delighted when, unable to keep away from you, I tracked you to your dinner with your father—*and* Dawson,' he added heavily. 'But you forgave me my churlishness and even defied your father by agreeing to meet me later. It was then that I really began to hope that you might be starting to care a little for me.'

Again Phelix came near to revealing her true feelings for him. But she knew that he must know anyway. Though—perhaps not, she realised in wonder, because all at once Nathan was looking at her very seriously. And when he spoke she suddenly knew that the time had come when for him—for his love and his vulnerability and his pride that she had so badly bruised—she must push through that final barrier.

'Once, up on that mountain, I offered you my heart. I meant it then. I mean it now.' He paused, and then, never more serious, 'Will you now take it, Phelix?'

Her heart thundered. He had told her he loved her, and she believed him. Incredible as it still seemed, he loved her—and she believed him. And she knew what he was asking.

'If you will take mine,' she replied, her voice barely audible. She thought then that he might draw her close. But he did not.

'Why?' he asked, his eyes steady on hers. Just that *why*, and nothing more.

'Because…' Her voice was cracking. 'Because…' She took a deep and steadying breath, and, her trust in him absolute, 'Because—I—love you, Nathan,' she said at last.

'Darling!' he breathed, and did not wait to hear any more, but held her tight up to him, tight up to his heart.

For ageless minutes they just held each other. Phelix's heart was full to overflowing to be held by Nathan, her love, to be able to hold him, her love, with no barriers.

The ringing of the telephone startled them apart. 'Ah—my father!' Nathan exclaimed. 'I was supposed to be meeting him.' He, albeit reluctantly, let her go. 'I'll be right back,' he said, and went to the bedside telephone. 'I'm sorry,' she heard him apologise. 'I'll—we'll be down in a few minutes.' There was a pause where Phelix guessed his father was querying that 'we,' and then Nathan's voice, joyous, as he told his father, 'Phelix has arrived—she's come to put me out of my misery.' Another pause, then Nathan was saying, 'See you shortly,' and replacing the phone and turning to her.

By then Phelix was on her feet. 'I—er…' she mumbled, feeling suddenly nervous.

Nathan came over to her and took her in his arms. 'I—er—nothing,' he said, placing a light kiss on the tip of her nose. 'I've told my father all about you—he can't wait to meet you.'

'You've told him?' she gasped.

Nathan smiled. 'On the flight over. He could see I was abstracted; he wanted to know what was troubling me—I told him of this beautiful girl I'd married, and how—'

'You told him you were married!'

Nathan looked at her sharply. 'You sound as if you'd rather I hadn't?'

'It's not that,' Phelix said quickly. 'It's just—my father said you'd told him you were going for a divorce as soon as you could. I just thought…'

'Stop thinking and listen to me,' Nathan instructed.

'You didn't tell my father…?'

'I did,' he owned. 'My stars, did he do his work well!' Nathan exclaimed in disgust. 'Hear me out, my darling. Your father was cock-a-hoop when he told me how you'd taken the first plane you could back to London. I wasn't going to let him see how devastated that made me, so I told him what had been in my mind anyway—that I couldn't wait to divorce you.'

'You're going for a divorce?' she asked quietly.

'Not now!' Nathan stressed in no uncertain fashion. '*Then* I was of the view that, with your father attempting to taint everything, I would end this marriage that had begun with him pulling the strings, and then I'd spend the following three months hopefully getting you to care enough for me, to marry me, *for me*—nothing to do with him.'

'You want to marry me?' Phelix asked, startled.

'That was before Saturday. That was before I made you mine, my darling. Ever since then I have regarded you as my wife, the other half of me. I can't divorce you now, Mrs Mallory,' he added softly. 'You are now a part of me,' he said tenderly, going on, 'What we can do, if you'd care to, is to renew our vows—with love.'

Phelix was feeling all choked-up and misty-eyed. 'You really want to stay married to me?' she whispered.

'There is no way you're getting away from me now, Phelix Mallory,' he answered firmly, but asked quickly, 'You don't want to, do you? Get away from me?'

'Never,' she replied.

'Will you, then, my darling, stay married to me, come live with me?' he asked.

Her heart was thundering. Never had she known such joy. 'Oh, yes, Nathan,' she answered. 'Oh, yes.'

'Sweet darling,' he exclaimed, overjoyed, but decreed, 'One kiss, then you must come with me and say hello to your father-in-law.'

'Oh, Nathan,' she sighed. 'I'd love to meet him.'

That one kiss became two, and Phelix's brain was away with the fairies when Nathan, with a most loving look to her flushed face, made a determined effort and, keeping one arm about her, turned her purposefully towards the door.

'Er—I'd better—um—think about doing something about getting a room,' she plucked out of somewhere as she sought to concentrate her mind on matters other than what Nathan could do to her and how he could make her feel. 'I—' She broke off as Nathan stood back and looked at her just a mite incredulously. 'What?' she asked.

'Hmm, at the risk of not sparing your blushes, dear Phelix, this is a double room,' he reminded her. And, if she had not quite caught on, 'That bed over there is more than big enough for two. And—' he smiled lovingly into her eyes '—we *are* married, my love.'

'Oh!' The wave of warm colour to her face was instant. And, remembering the raptures of Nathan's lovemaking, 'Oh,' she whispered softly, dreamily.

And Nathan, seeing her response, was delighted. 'Care to share?' he offered tenderly.

'Please,' she answered huskily. 'Yes, please.'

* * * * *

Celebrate 60 years of pure reading pleasure with Harlequin®!
Silhouette® Romantic Suspense is celebrating with the glamour-filled, adrenaline-charged series LOVE IN 60 SECONDS *starting in April 2009.*
Six stories that promise to bring the glitz of Las Vegas, the danger of revenge, the mystery of a missing diamond, family scandals and ripped-from-the-headlines intrigue. Get your heart racing as love happens in sixty seconds!

Enjoy a sneak peek of
USA TODAY *bestselling author Marie Ferrarella's*
THE HEIRESS'S 2-WEEK AFFAIR
Available April 2009 from Silhouette® Romantic Suspense.

Eight years ago Matt Shaffer had vanished out of Natalie Rothchild's life, leaving behind a one-line note tucked under pillow that had grown cold: *I'm sorry, but this just isn't oing to work.*

That was it. No explanation, no real indication of remorse. The note had been as clinical and compassionless as an eviction otice, which, in effect, it had been, Natalie thought as she navgated through the morning traffic. Matt had written the note o evict her from his life.

She'd spent the next two weeks crying, breaking down without warning as she walked down the street, or as she sat taring at a meal she couldn't bring herself to eat.

Candace, she remembered with a bittersweet pang, had tried o get her to go clubbing in order to get her to forget about Matt.

She'd turned her twin down, but she did get her act together. f Matt didn't think enough of their relationship to try to contact er, to try to make her understand why he'd changed so radially from lover to stranger, then to hell with him. He was dead o her, she resolved. And he'd remained that way.

Until twenty minutes ago.

The adrenaline in her veins kept mounting.

Natalie focused on her driving. Vegas in the daylight wasn't early as alluring, as magical and glitzy as it was after dark.

Like an aging woman best seen in soft lighting, Vegas's imperfections were all visible in the daylight. Natalie supposed that was why people like her sister didn't like to get up until noon. They lived for the night.

Except that Candace could no longer do that.

The thought brought a fresh, sharp ache with it.

"Damn it, Candy, what a waste," Natalie murmured under her breath.

She pulled up before the Janus casino. One of the three valets currently on duty came to life and made a beeline for her vehicle.

"Welcome to the Janus," the young attendant said cheerfully as he opened her door with a flourish.

"We'll see," she replied solemnly.

As he pulled away with her car, Natalie looked up at the casino's logo. Janus was the Roman god with two faces, one pointed toward the past, the other facing the future. It struck her as rather ironic, given what she was doing here, seeking out someone from her past in order to get answers so that the future could be settled.

The moment she entered the casino, the Vegas phenomena took hold. It was like stepping into a world where time did not matter or even make an appearance. There was only a sense of "now."

Because in Natalie's experience she'd discovered that bartenders knew the inner workings of any establishment they worked for better than anyone else, she made her way to the first bar she saw within the casino.

The bartender in attendance was a gregarious man in his early forties. He had a quick, sexy smile, which was probably one of the main reasons he'd been hired. His name tag identified him as Kevin.

Moving to her end of the bar, Kevin asked, "What'll it be, pretty lady?"

"Information." She saw a dubious look cross his brow. To

ounter that, she took out her badge. Granted she wasn't here an official capacity, but Kevin didn't need to know that. Were you on duty last night?"

Kevin began to wipe the gleaming black surface of the bar. You mean during the gala?"

"Yes."

The smile gracing his lips was a satisfied one. Last night had bviously been profitable for him, she judged. "I caught an xtra shift."

She took out Candace's photograph and carefully placed it n the bar. "Did you happen to see this woman there?"

The bartender glanced at the picture. Mild interest turned to cognition. "You mean Candace Rothchild? Yeah, she was ere, loud and brassy as always. But not for long," he added, oking rather disappointed. There was always a circus when andace was around, Natalie thought. "She and the boss had t it and then he had our head of security escort her out."

She latched onto the first part of his statement. "They rgued? About what?"

He shook his head. "Couldn't tell you. Too far away for nything but body language," he confessed.

"And the head of security?" she asked.

"He got her to leave."

She leaned in over the bar. "Tell me about him."

"Don't know much," the bartender admitted. "Just that his ame's Matt Shaffer. Boss flew him in from L.A., where he was ead of security for Montgomery Enterprises."

There was no avoiding it, she thought darkly. She was going have to talk to Matt. The thought left her cold. "Do you know here I can find him right now?"

Kevin glanced at his watch. "He should be in his office. On e second floor, toward the rear." He gave her the numbers of e rooms where the monitors that kept watch over the casino uests as they tried their luck against the house were located.

Taking out a twenty, she placed it on the bar. "Thanks for your help."

Kevin slipped the bill into his vest pocket. "Any time, lovely lady," he called after her. "Any time."

She debated going up the stairs, then decided on the elevator The car that took her up to the second floor was empty. Natalie stepped out of the elevator, looked around to get her bearing and then walked toward the rear of the floor.

"Into the Valley of Death rode the six hundred," she silently recited, digging deep for a line from a poem by Tennyson Wrapping her hand around a brass handle, she opened one of the glass doors and walked in.

The woman whose desk was closest to the door looked up "You can't come in here. This is a restricted area."

Natalie already had her ID in her hand and held it up. "I'm looking for Matt Shaffer," she told the woman.

God, even saying his name made her mouth go dry. She was supposed to be over him, to have moved on with her life What happened?

The woman began to answer her. "He's—"

"Right here."

The deep voice came from behind her. Natalie felt every single nerve ending go on tactical alert at the same moment that all the hairs at the back of her neck stood up. Eight years had passed, but she would have recognized his voice anywhere.

* * * * *

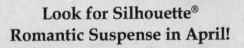

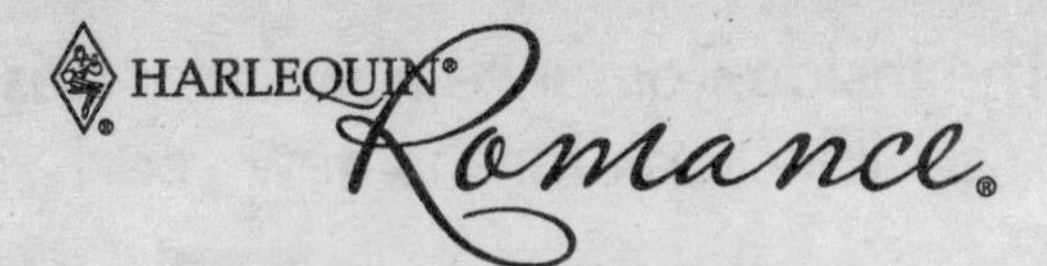

Coming Next Month

Available April 14, 2009

This month Harlequin Romance® brings you a new story by *New York Times* bestselling author Diana Palmer, and the start of can't-miss trilogy *www.blinddatebrides.com!*

#4087 DIAMOND IN THE ROUGH Diana Palmer
A brand-new story from ***The Men of Medicine Ridge.*** When Sassy discovers that cowboy John is secretly a millionaire, she thinks he's just been playing with her. John must convince Sassy that he's the man she first thought he was—a diamond in the rough.

#4088 THE COWBOY AND THE PRINCESS Myrna Mackenzie
Western Weddings
When reclusive rancher Owen is asked to look after defiant Princess Delfyne, he can't say no. He *should* say no—Delfyne is regal, gorgeous and betrothed to another man!

#4089 SECRET BABY, SURPRISE PARENTS Liz Fielding
Baby on Board
Grace told herself that surrogacy for her sister was selfless, but she secretly longed for the baby to be her own. Josh wished they were his to take care of. When tragedy struck, would Josh claim them as his family?

#4090 NINE-TO-FIVE BRIDE Jennie Adams
Marissa joined ***www.blinddatebrides.com*** for a bit of fun! Her sexy new boss Rick was more Mr. Tall, Dark and Dangerous than Mr. Right. Marissa would never date him…would she?

#4091 THE REBEL KING Melissa James
When fireman Charlie finds himself ***Suddenly Royal!,*** he rebels! But his bad-boy act doesn't fool Princess Jazmine. She knows he is kind, generous and fit to be king!

#4092 MARRYING THE MANHATTAN MILLIONAIRE Jackie Braun
9 to 5
Successful executive Samantha's ex-fiancé and business rival, Michael, is back! And the real merger on the table is more than strictly business….

HRCNMBPA0309